Primal Claim

The Sigma Menace: Book 2

By Marie Johnston

GW00809035

Primal Claim

After losing her family to feral shifters, Dani dedicated her life to eradicating those responsible, almost reaching Agent status with Sigma. Uncertainty about the network, and questions about their purpose were plaguing her when she was tasked with a mission that would forever change her and send her running toward those she once sought to destroy.

Mercury's past and unique looks kept him distant from people, including those of his own species. Then he captured a beautiful Sigma recruit who claimed to need his help while her scent claimed to be carrying his young.

Bitter enemies brought together, they must rely on each other to keep Sigma from getting their hands on Dani, or the growing life inside of her.

To my kids. They make me feel young, yet very old, at the same time.

Chapter One

"Of course, Madame G," Dani said, head bowed, hands clasped in front of her. She had been elevated past the rank of being on her knees in front of the dark mistress like a recruit, but not yet promoted to Agent status. Madame G had one more mission for her. Dani formed her next sentence carefully. "I would do anything to rid the world of the shifter threat."

Dani resisted the urge to squirm under the menacing woman's scrutiny. *Batshit crazy*. Wasn't the first time those words rose up in Dani's mind as Madame G stood before her in a long kimono that covered every inch of skin except for her smooth, porcelain face. It also wasn't the first time Dani questioned her determination in the destruction of all shifter kind. Her *kill them all resolve* had changed to well, maybe kill just the really bad ones. But it wasn't as if she could say, "My bad. I'm just gonna head back home." In the Sigma Network, there was no retirement, no pension plan, no severance package. You were killed in the line of duty or by Madame G herself. Save for the random training accident, that was it—no quitting.

"But to rid the world," Madame G purred cryptically, "what if you needed to first bring one into the world?"

"What?" Dani's head whipped up, but once she looked into the cold, black depths of the head mistress's eyes, she immediately bowed her head again. "My apologies. I'm only seeking to understand."

"I need a shifter's baby and I have a good feeling about you. I think you may just have it in you to conceive and carry one to term."

Dani swallowed hard. Her? Have a baby? A *shifter's* baby?

"I—wha—how?" She stuttered, eyes intent on the floor but seeing nothing.

"Oh my dear. Worry not. We have obtained the seed and prepped it for insemination." Madame G cooed before the steel returned to her voice. "I want it done tonight."

"Tonight?" Dani echoed.

"Yes. Drink this, my dear." Madame G's pale, elegant hand shoved a chalice under Dani's nose. It smelled like wine, but with her mistress, nothing was as it seemed. When she offered food and drink, it was for her benefit only. And you never, ever wanted Madame G to offer you anything to ingest.

"Drink," she commanded again, her voice dropping a chilling octave.

Fear drove Dani to grab the glass, avoiding any skin-to-skin contact with the dark lady, and down it before any thoughts brought further hesitation. Delay would only make the inevitable more painful.

The acrid wine burned its way down Dani's throat, her mind reeling. She handed the cup back to Madame G as she bowed her head again. The brief moment her eyes hit Madame G's face, she took in the smug greed that filled it. A *baby*? She was supposed to be inseminated and somehow conceive. Tonight? Who even knew where she was in her monthly cycle? What would happen to her if she didn't conceive?

Madame G snapped her fingers and the door open behind Dani.

"Enter, Agent T." Footsteps approached upon Madame G's command.

Well, this didn't make the situation any better. Agent T was a douche. Dani avoided him as much as possible, managing to get other Agents to help her carry out her vengeance against shifter kind. It was over and done with, really. She had personally hunted down and disposed of those responsible for her family's violent and tragic deaths. Hence her personal dilemma of remaining with Sigma, after seeing how their definition of justice differed from hers.

The few times Agent T was in charge of Dani's training, she felt like she needed a shower after being in his presence. He used any excuse to touch her, his fingers lingering past the awkward stage. Not to mention she knew his habits outside of missions. He liked visiting the seduction-training ladies, but claimed they bored him. He could often be found when he was off duty, trolling the clubs and bars looking for new conquests. One day he showed up with two black eyes. Rumor was that he had hit on Agent X. Dani smirked every time she imagined how that played out.

Dani's stomach roiled, the wine wasn't settling well at all. Or whatever was in the wine wasn't settling well. Her body flushed and burned hot all over. What was in that wine?

"Daniella." Madame G never used her nickname. Dani had wondered what letter she'd be assigned when she became an Agent and with the death of the last Agent D, she thought maybe "D" would be hers. Would Madame G still insist on calling her Daniella? She really hated hearing her full name on that woman's lips. "You should be in your fertile state, but just in case, I had the lab refine the hormone dose we use to boost fertility."

Awww, hell. Dani heard about the fertility booster Madame G was developing. A couple of months ago, it had been used on a shifter's mate. It may or may not have boosted her fertility, but reports came back that the recipient had gone from being on fire with desire, to tossing her cookies, repeatedly. Dani was hot now, her stomach upset, her head starting to swim, leaving little room for any desire to set in.

"Go with Agent T now. I asked him to make sure you enjoy it, it might help your body accept the seed."

Dani was about to turn and run, damn the consequences, but her reflexes were slowing, her vision blurring. Agent T grabbed her arms and hauled her out of Madame G's luxurious office.

"Let me go," Dani managed to slur. She heard the bastard chuckle at her efforts.

"Agent T, remember my warning," Madame G intoned.

"Yes ma'am," he said, dragging Dani into the elevator.

Dani passed out in the elevator. She regained consciousness briefly to Agent T carrying her down into the bowels of the building. The lower levels of Sigma's Freemont training center were below ground where they housed the Agents, training facilities, and part of Madame G's laboratories. Her lab-based testing was on one of the above-ground floors, but her specimen-based testing was underground where it could be secured better. And where noise, like screaming, could be muffled from the outside.

Agent T carried her into one of the smaller rooms that contained nothing but a sink, a syringe, and an examining table.

Struggling weakly only increased her dizziness and she passed out again.

Cool air wafting over her breasts brought Dani around again. Fuzzy-headed, she looked down to her bare chest and stomach. Someone lifted her legs into the stirrups attached to the examining bed.

Kicking out, she freed one leg, only for it to fall with a clang against the table.

A man's soft snicker brought her head up as much as she possibly could. Her body felt like lead, like molten lead, it burned so hot.

"Oh God," she moaned.

"Sssh, I'll make it feel good." Agent T captured her leg again, bringing it up into the stirrups.

"No!" She struggled, as strongly as a newborn kitten. "Don't touch me!"

"But that's all I can do or Madame G will burn my junk off. She wants no doubt about paternity." Agent T finished restraining her ankles and slid a stool over to sit between her legs. "But you'll enjoy being inseminated. Trust me."

A wave of revulsion coursed through her, her stomach heaved, and she used all her might to try to push herself off the table, only to make her head swim and lose consciousness yet once more.

**

"What's wrong, Merc?"

Mercury shook his head, sweat droplets flying through the air.

"I don't know. I just feel…" He shook his head again and turned toward Bennett Young, his partner, and continued sparring. Bennett lunged for him while another Guardian came up from behind to grab him in a chokehold. Which was completely successful because Mercury stopped to gaze northeast again, toward where Freemont sprawled across the river. They couldn't see it from where their headquarters lay south of West Creek. The lodge was settled deep into the woods and that was where the Guardians lived and trained.

"Distracted as hell?" Jace Stockwell finished for him as he released his hold on his neck. Bennett loved giving Jace shit for taking his human mate, Cassie's, last name. Jace argued that his last name was a generic filler so it fit him, while Bennett argued that shit like that just wasn't done in his day, which was quite a long time ago. Mercury didn't have a last name, unwilling to carry a generic moniker that didn't mean anything. If his name wasn't so fittingly descriptive, it'd have no meaning to him, either. When Master Bellamy found him all those decades ago, he had to call him something, and with his silver gleaming black hair and black eyes that reflected silver pools, "Mercury" it was.

"I just feel…" Mercury drifted off again, looking northeast, searching for anything that would give him an answer. "Like I'm needed somewhere."

"The Den?" Bennett asked sarcastically.

Mercury shook his head. He'd pretty much given up that outlet. It'd been months. Bennett quit going, trying therapy with Cassie instead. Jace's mate was a psychologist they'd rescued, along with her best friend Kaitlyn, who was also a Guardian now. The Guardians had known Jace from his bartending gig at Pale Moonlight and were eyeballing him for recruitment when Sigma captured him and his mate. Once they were rescued and reunited, Jace joined the Guardians and Cassie became part of their odd family.

"No, just like… someone needs my help." Who could that be? He didn't have anyone outside his Guardian circle. His past made it difficult for him to socialize and associate with people. He didn't fully understand social nuances, said what was on his mind, and was accused of being too blunt. Bennett hated that he picked up the dialogues and sayings of the times and in Bennett's words "abused the hell out of them."

Bennett shook his head in confusion. "Who?"

"Yeah," was all Mercury could say. He stripped down. "I gotta run."

"You need backup?" Jace asked. Mercury knew either male had his back, but Jace felt obliged as Mercury shadowed his mate several times on her runs when Jace couldn't go with her. It's not like it was hard. She only had two legs.

"No." He was off.

The feeling continued, unabated, for weeks. Mercury ran every day, searching. Someone was out there and they needed him.

Chapter Two

Dani lay in the bed in her tiny dorm-like room. It had been almost two weeks since the procedure. She considered it assault.

She didn't know what had happened specifically as she only gained random moments of lucidity. She at least knew that Madame G terrified Agent T enough that he kept his "junk" away from her. She remembered that he wasn't concerned with covering her when he carried her unceremoniously to her room, dumped her on her bed, gave her a lewd wink, and left.

Once enough strength had returned, Dani crawled to the shower and sat under the spray for an hour. On autopilot, she finally shut the water off, half-heartedly toweled off, and put on the thickest pants and sweater she could find. With every light in the room on, she burrowed far under her covers and made a pathetic attempt at sleep.

But her mind wouldn't shut off. For days Dani stayed in a near zombie state, rousing only to nibble at some crackers, sip tepid water, and go to the bathroom. The rest of the time she used to think. Think about her past, present, and future. And plan.

After the first week had passed, Agent X started coming to her. First, to make sure Dani ate at least once a day. While she forced food down, loathe to even taste it, X would prattle on about the latest Agent gossip. If Dani had to label an Agent as friend, it'd be X. They weren't close exactly, but in this fucked-up world created by Madame G, she respected the hell out of X. She knew nothing about the rocker chick other than she was a shifter and they had similar histories—Dani's family was wiped out by rogue shifters, and X's family was wiped out by an unknown entity. At least unknown to everyone else. Dani had a feeling X knew who was responsible and they would eventually be made to pay.

The second reason X came to her room was to escort her to the weekly lab visits. For now, all the mad doctor wanted from her was her blood. A quick draw to test for insemination success. It was more sensitive than urine, they said. And more painful, probably why they preferred it.

The first week's results were inconclusive.

A knock on the door told Dani that week two's results were being greatly anticipated.

"Open the fuck up, doll," X called from the other side.

In spite of her dire situation, Dani smiled. She really was fond of the convivial Agent. Unlike many of the other Agents, X and her partner Agent E were not mindless followers of Madame G. They didn't target just any shifters, mostly ones like the feral pack that took out Dani's family. Both of whom they helped Dani hunt and put down, training her in the process. Otherwise, their main mission had to do with keeping the Guardians distracted, and Dani bet there was some juicy history there.

The grin quickly faded as Dani swung her legs down and ambled toward the door. Swinging it open, she faced the female on the other side. X's hair was as short as Dani's was long and slightly darker. The style of the day was Elvis, slicked up with the swirl hanging down onto her forehead. X's stunning green eyes always caught Dani a little off guard—dead serious, but with an air of mischievousness.

X cocked an eyebrow. "Ready, my little recruit bitch?"

"Let's do it." They headed down the hall to the elevator.

"Pos or neg? Wanna make a bet? Do your tits hurt? I heard that's the first sign. Puking?" X waited for Dani to shake her head. "Nope. Hmmm, I'm gonna go with negative. But what do I know? The lunk's baby juice could be superpowered."

"Wait. What? Do you know the shifter they used?" Lunk? A flash of irritation flitted through Dani.

X raised her eyebrows. "You mean they didn't tell you? Oh doll, I'll fill you in as soon as we get back. I gotta meet Biggie in an hour, so we have time."

Numbly, Dani nodded her head. "Biggie" was what X called her partner, Agent E. "Get it? Big E," X had chortled when Dani asked why she called him that. Not knowing just how closely the Agents worked together, Dani wasn't sure she really got it.

The elevator chimed and they went inside. Ten minutes and a little bit of blood later, they had their answer.

Dani knew it would be positive. Not because her "tits" hurt or because she was constantly nauseous. She just knew. She knew a life grew inside of her and despite her best attempts at ignoring it, at rejecting the idea that Madame G's demented plan would take root, the little curl of warmth slipped through her mind and burrowed in.

Her moods had changed. Weren't pregnant ladies moody? Her determination to leave was solidifying, her anger at those involved in the conception was growing, and when X said she knew who the unwitting sperm donor was, she wanted to shove her against the wall, blade at her throat, and demand every morsel of information. Except with X, Dani would likely end up on her back on the floor, with a blade already cutting skin at her own throat.

X shadowed Dani out of the lab and back to the elevator after the mad doctor rattled off the list of instructions for the expectant mother. The primary one being that she couldn't leave the facility's grounds "for safety reasons" because "she's so important." Dani just wanted to grab X's arm and haul her down to her rooms so she could find out about her baby's sperm donor.

Turning the corner to the elevator, Dani almost groaned when she saw the fangbanger waiting for a ride. The "sexual artist" in charge of seduction training and vampire blood feedings was always annoying, but today Dani couldn't stand the sight of Janice's bottle-job red hair and cutsie outfits.

"He-ey," Janice called as they drew closer. "Dani, right? Are you the one carrying the shifter's young?"

Suppressing a growl—*growl?*—Dani refrained from pointing out that it was her baby, too. Not Madame G's, not the mad doctor's with the eager smile, not the shifter's. It was hers.

"'Sup, Janice?" X asked, irritation lacing her tone.

The elevator doors opened and they filed in.

"Hey, Agent X," Janice greeted, then turned to Dani. "I was always wondering how you got out of participating in my training. I bet they wanted to save you for that male's baby."

The lusty redhead fanned her ample bosom and kept going, oblivious to the lack of interest in her presence.

"My word," Janice drawled. "Between you and me, it's been a little boring here for me since that mission. Those males... so virile. And their stamina... oooh."

Blood began to pound in Dani's ears. Her heartbeat thudding strongly as she put two and two together.

"What did you do for the mission?" Dani asked tightly.

"What didn't I do," Janice panted, and kicked her hip out. "Let me tell you, the one they had me steal the product from, the weird one, he could go all night. And *big*. It's a good thing you didn't have to get pregnant by him the old-fashioned way. Giiiirl, he'd a broke you."

Anger built on top of anger for a reason Dani couldn't understand, and this woman needed to shut the fuck up. But as the elevator door opened, she kept talking.

"I sucked him off so long, I should've gotten a gallon of cum. But I had to be sneaky."

Must. Not. Throat. Punch. It was like a sledgehammer was hitting her brain and reverberating through her chest, her blood pulsed through her. As they neared the corner where they would hopefully part ways, Janice turned to what she must've felt was an avid audience and continued. By now Dani was breathing heavy, like a bull ready to charge, glaring at Janice through lowered lids.

"It's just not the same here. The new recruits are inexperienced with someone of my vast skills. The others… been there, done that." Janice leaned in closer, speaking to X who had come to a stop next to Dani, and whispered conspiratorially. "I'm going back to Pale Moonlight. I mean, those shifters don't know what happened. I just *need* one more night. To wrap my mouth around his—"

Dani's fist whipped out and throat-punched the woman. There was no thought, just action. Not even X saw it coming. Janice dropped to the floor, choking, grabbing her throat.

"Oh my god! What did I do?" Clarity rushed back. Dani stepped back, watching Janice writhe on the floor, struggling to draw in a breath. Sure, she'd killed before, but not an innocent. Well, Janice wasn't exactly innocent but Dani didn't know if she deserved to be watched while suffocating on the floor.

Dani looked at X, who gazed back impassively, waiting for Dani's reaction.

"Shouldn't we save her?" Dani asked, yet neither one made a move to do so.

X shrugged and looked back down at Janice, whose bulging eyes were pleading with X to help her. "I don't know. You gonna miss someone who lures doped out young girls at the clubs to come here and be blood feeders and fangbangers?"

Blood feeders were the blood supply for the vampire Agents at Sigma. Dani had heard Madame G even had a few vampires she kept for her studies and they required blood feeders also. Those poor girls were usually the most strung out, too far gone of the batch. And they rarely came back from the feedings. It was better for them if they didn't survive. Sane vampires could seduce the blood from their prey, but vampires kept for lab experiments weren't often sane.

"I knew I never liked her," Dani replied.

Not looking forward to watching a person die a slow, painful death, especially one she caused, Dani was relieved when X used her booted foot to fling Janice's hands off her throat and stepped down until the *sexual artist's* air was completely cut off. It was only a matter of moments before the woman went completely still, her eyes vacant and fixed.

"Besides, doll, she was just telling us she planned to disobey orders and jeopardize Mission Baby." X flipped out her radio and spoke into it. "Clean up, aisle 5."

Once X was done radioing directions to recruits, she turned to head toward Dani's room.

"Did I understand her right?" Dani rushed after. "The shifter they got for the… stuff, he hangs out at Pale Moonlight?"

"Yep."

"Is he… "

"Yep."

Fuck. A Guardian. Her sperm donor is not only *a* Guardian, he's one of *those* Guardians. One of the pack that frequents the infamous back rooms in the shifter-owned club Pale Moonlight. Dani had heard many tales of what went on in The Den, especially about the three Guardians who liked to play together with their women in one of those rooms. And now she was carrying the baby of one of them.

"Look, doll. I gotta jet and tell Madame G that I have to replace her seduction trainer. They were getting sick of her, anyway. 'Loose and flappy' was Agent W's description. That vamp cracks me up. Any hoodels, you gotta be dying of curiosity so here's the run down. He's kinda weird."

Not quite what Dani was expecting, but the unexpected insult toward the baby daddy started the low thrum in her head again. What was going on with her?

"He's hot as hell, don't get me wrong. They all are. His looks are… unique. If you ever see him, you'll know why they call him Mercury. Helluva fighter, if I have to give a damn Guardian a compliment. Just seems a little… slow. Don't know what his issue is, but we all got one. Am I right?" X clapped her shoulder and opened the door for Dani, who hadn't noticed they already reached her room. She wandered in and turned back to X.

"How did Madame G know that he and I could produce an interspecies young? Don't they have to mate first?"

The underlying seriousness that was always there suddenly dominated X's face.

"No mating required for baby making. I have no idea how she gets the information she does. It's not through natural means. Can you imagine what she'll do with a baby?" X turned to go and then turned back. "It's a good thing those wolves don't know what you carry. They're protective as hell so imagine what a Guardian would be like.

You'd be on lockdown with all of them protecting that little bundle of furry joy." Shaking her head, X sauntered off.

Dani let the door fall shut, but continued to stare at it. She knew what she had to do.

Chapter Three

Lying in bed, plans that were started during those dark days after her assault began cementing in her mind. Her Plan A needed to have a Plan B and C, and be meticulous. Madame G would keep close tabs on her now that she was the only successful interspecies insemination. Dani wasn't naïve. There'd been more attempts. There had to have been. While she was off with Agent X and Agent E, hunting the bastards that killed her family, there were demented Agents that hunted and kidnapped innocents only because they were shifters. Dani didn't know what Madame G did with the captives, but she heard enough screams, enough hushed conversations, to know it wasn't good.

At first, she'd convinced herself that those creatures crying in despair were guilty of the same crimes she'd witnessed those feral shifters carry out. Later, after more interaction with the recruits and Agents, Dani realized there were few under Sigma's umbrella that joined with her same righteous intentions of forever protecting the innocent. Most joined because of their intense hatred of paranormals, unless they were a vampire, then their hatred was aimed at shifters. Many joined because they wanted a license to kill, anyone or anything—didn't matter.

Still needing one light left on in the room, Dani drifted off.

A faint sound woke her. What was it? A click? Rustling?

Someone's in here with me. Grateful she took advice from X and got used to sleeping armed with at least one knife, her hand crept under the blankets until it wrapped around the hilt. Slowly, she opened her eyes.

The room was completely dark. Fear sizzled up her spine. *I wish a light was on!*

Her bedside lamp flickered on.

Her gaze landed instantly on the form that stood at the edge of her bed. Agent T's face registered the shock of the light turning on.

"I can't get your smell out of my head," he rasped.

"You should've gotten enough of it a couple of weeks ago," she said through clenched teeth.

"There wasn't much I *could* do. Couldn't fuck you. Tried to play with you, but you kept passing out."

Her stomach roiled at the few memories she did have of that day. So, he was back for more.

"I heard the news. Congratulations, by the way. Before you get big and bloated with that freak you're carrying, I need to have you. I'll keep my promise that you'll enjoy it."

"I *seriously* doubt that." The thrumming returned. He insulted her baby. Rage began to build. This man *insulted* her baby. He assaulted her, copping feels, attempting more, and now he thought he could rape her in her own bed.

Fuck. That.

"I need to have you." Agent T lunged for her. Dani came up, snapping her knife out, aiming for a vital spot on his body.

He was too fast for her, hitting her arm out of the way. She almost lost the grip on her knife, but managed to keep hold of it. He grabbed her arms and pinned them above her head as she bucked wildly beneath him.

Unfortunately, his size and fighting experience overpowered her quickly. Agent T used his free hand to snatch away the blankets while his large body immobilized hers. She continued to struggle, frantically looking around her room for something, anything, she could use against him. Nothing but her lamp and some books, but no free hands to grab at them.

He ripped her tank top open and grappled at her shorts. Hot breath drifted over her breasts, his mouth too close. She spotted one of her old college textbooks. More ripping fabric and her bottom half would be open to him.

I wish I could smash his head with a book.

A heavy, thick book came flying off the shelf and slammed into Agent T's skull. With an *oomph*, he fell to her side. Yanking her hands free, the knife still clutched tightly, she swiftly brought it across the most vulnerable spot she could find, his throat.

Hot blood sprayed her. Agent T gurgled, grabbed at his throat futilely to stanch the blood flow. A sense of déjà vu hit her. Another throat attack, she was two for two. She scrambled from the bed and spun on him. Agent T grabbed for his sidearm but his blood-coated hands were too slippery to get a good grip.

Dani slapped his hands away and shoved him on his back; he was weakening rapidly. Climbing on top of him to pin him down, she made sure he couldn't grab at any more weapons, then leaned down close where he gaped like a hooked fish.

"Don't worry," she hissed. "I'll make sure you enjoy this." Dani waited until the last bit of life drained out of him.

***

Mercury sat straight up in bed. His bed, in this case, was the floor. He'd only moved inside in the last thirty years, uncomfortable with a roof over his head. It'd be another thirty years before he slept on an actual bed. They were just so *soft*.

He walked around all day feeling like something momentous had happened. But what? It was business as usual at the lodge. Kaitlyn was in the final phase of her training. Her youth and vitality were a breath of fresh air. The search for her true paternity was a welcome change to the daily grind. Jace was adapting to their brotherhood nicely and Cassie, his human mate, seemed happy living deep in the woods. Mercury thought it was nice to be around the mated couple, seeing them laughing and chatting, looking for any excuse to touch. Mercury's missions usually took them to families devastated by Sigma or the dregs of their society—feral shifters that turned on humans or their own kind.

Not everyone at the lodge got a little mood boost from the new arrivals. Mason Ternes, in charge of security and their IT support, was becoming progressively withdrawn. He went down to the club for sex more and more frequently, ignoring Commander Fitzsimmons' and Bennett's warnings. Mason was always an asshole, but his moods continued to grow darker, and his lack of respect toward those they helped in the field was concerning. It was convenient that modern times brought rapidly changing technology—it kept Mason busy with cameras, computers, and firepower, and away from society.

The twins, Malcolm and Harrison Wallace, continued to do their own thing, barely contained by the commander. They got along well enough with the other Guardians, but had not yet accepted them as the family they felt like to Mercury. Master Bellamy, the retired Guardian who trained and mentored them all, was the father figure Mercury never had.

Otherwise, nothing had changed except the feeling that someone needed him. Now.

Not bothering with any clothes, Mercury walked out the door and let his beast run.

***

Sometimes they come back. That was a Sigma inside joke. Only it really wasn't. Was Agent T enhanced enough to survive a throat slitting? It didn't matter. Even if Dani dragged him to the bathtub, she couldn't burn his body without drawing way too much attention. No one could be alerted because right now, fuck Plans A, B, and C. Sleazy Agent T dropped Plan A-plus right in her lap. Literally.

As much as Dani wanted to shower the blood stains of Agent T off her, she needed to be covered in his blood. Just not as much of it. Not that she wanted to rush to the bathroom, strip down, and shower while a dead Agent was in her bed. So instead, she washed off her hands and face, gave her hair a quick rinse and then put it in ponytail.

His blood was her freedom. And his finger? She'd get that after she packed. Rummaging through her drawers, she threw on her tactical pants and a fitted long-sleeved black shirt. After donning her boots, she proceeded to load up with every weapon she could possibly carry. Unfortunately, it wasn't much as she hadn't been promoted yet. Full Agents could own whatever they wanted. Recruits were given only the basics, nothing that couldn't be defended against by the Agents if a recruit needed putting down. Dani was somewhere in between. Two guns and five knives were much better than nothing. She took what she could pilfer off Agent T's body, which wasn't much as he wasn't loaded for a mission. His goal had been to finish what he'd started before with her, so he only carried the bare minimum. After strapping her gear in place, she wiped off only the handle of the knife she took Agent T down with.

Dead men were heavy. Completely limp and malleable. Grunting and cursing, Dani wrestled with Agent T until she could cut away and strip off lightly-coated fabric from his blood-soaked shirt to stuff in her pocket. A little extra scent never hurt.

Next, she rummaged through his pockets looking for his keys. After stuffing them into another pocket, she drew her knife once more and grabbed the Agent's limp forearm, separating his right index finger from the rest. *And this isn't the worst I've done.* She mused while she sawed away at the digit at the one-eighty her life had taken from a privileged, well-respected member of society to a hardened mercenary on the run.

Madame G's other drones may not be watching her that closely yet, since she just received the news of her expectant status. They may not even be sure that she'd jet as soon as possible, only that she and her baby-on-board needed to be protected, and that most likely included limiting her excursions into town. There was no doubt, however, if they had any inkling she wanted to cut ties with Sigma and leave, that she would become the most locked down, without-hope prisoner that was there.

Agent X was a shifter and had all their heightened senses. The human enhanced Agents, like Agent E, also had heightened senses and increased speed. Dani was human. As much as she respected the two Agents, Dani didn't trust them with ensuring her freedom. They may turn the other way when they saw normal shifters going about their lives, they may not have used unnecessary violence when dispatching feral shifters and insane bloodsuckers, but they at least did the minimum necessary to stay under Madame G's radar. Madame G employed enough mindless killers, so she utilized X and E's highly-skilled ways to further her own agenda, not to fuel her avid joy in slaughter and mayhem. No, X and E would not be alive if they did things like let the vessel carrying the coveted shifter baby go free.

Escape came back to the fact that Dani was human. If she passed other Agents in the garages, they'd question her immediately. Recruits didn't own vehicles and couldn't drive unless they were issued a vehicle for a mission. She'd have no business in the garages. Her only hope would be to remain unseen. But to do so, she had to give off the least human scent as possible. Recruits weren't granted any access to the loading bays without an Agent escort and she had to go through those to get to the garages. She knew Agent T's obnoxious red Mustang sat in one of the bays, hence the reason for the index finger. Dani was grateful that the secure areas hadn't been upgraded to retinal scans yet. Sometimes, it was the small things.

Straightening up, Dani wrapped the finger in another little scrap of cloth she'd cut off to carry it in. It seemed less gross than shoving it in her pocket, plus she didn't want to damage the print impressions on it. She fervently hoped the blood that covered her wouldn't be too fragrant, but masked her scent adequately. If some of her scent remained, she trusted the gossip channels running through the compound. Many would assume that after his help during insemination, Agent T finally got a piece of her.

A deep breath and quick mental run through the new and improved (and only) escape plan, Dani was ready. Opening the door a crack, she put her ear close to the opening. It was after midnight in a compound of night creatures. Agents would either be sleeping because they had day missions or were out for the night, but vampire Agents could be roaming. Recruits still trained during the day and any on field assignments would be out. She'd have to stay away from training gyms, the most likely spot to find anyone at this time of night.

Hearing nothing, Dani crept out. Heart pounding, she carefully maneuvered the hallways.

For three years, she'd been relieved to evade the enhancements Madame G assigned to those humans who were to become Agents. Oh, there was the curiosity about why, but her new status as the vessel for shifter babies answered some of her questions. At this moment, though, Dani wished for at least one heightened sense. But then she remembered the light she wished on, and the book she wished would slam Agent T's head—one wish and done. All in her imagination? Did she somehow get three wishes and had only one left?

No time to wonder. Time to get the fuck out. Dani made it to the stairs. Most residents of Sigma's compound used the elevator. The stairs were dark and creepy, and poorly maintained. No matter how badass anyone here thought they'd become, they still avoided the stairs.

As nimbly as she could, she took the stairs two at a time, getting it over with as quickly as possible. Glowing lights flickered along the walls, casting shadows along them. The faint sickly, sweet odor of death lingered, leaving those who braved the passage to ponder just who met their fate here, how long ago, and if were they still haunting the stairwell.

By the time Dani reached the top, she thought her heart was going to pound out of her chest. At least she was close to the loading bays. The garages were on the other side of the brightly lit, wide open loading bay. Damn.

Dani peered through the rectangular window in the door, she couldn't see or hear anyone. Digging Agent T's digit out of her pocket, she pressed it onto the scanner quickly before any second thoughts had her wondering if this was really going to work. Metal clunking inside the door told her it had and she crept inside.

The bays were mostly empty tonight. Unfortunately, that left her with a lot of realty to cross without the benefit of cover. Dani crept silently along the wall in the direction of the garages, attempting to stay out of sight, but trying not to look like she was sneaking around. If her impromptu escape plan was successful, whoever was on security detail that night would be dead by morning. Everyone in that branch of Sigma knew about Madame G's obsession with shifter babies and her maniacal drive to produce one for her own use. Dani suspected Madame G had practiced on herself many times over the years, using many different methods before searching for a suitable vessel to impregnate.

Dani heard voices before she heard the click of the secure door to one of the training gyms unlock. Darting behind a stack of boxes on a pallet, she crouched low hoping to remain unseen. Only one of the gyms opened to the loading bay instead of locker rooms. Agents wanting to take a short cut to the lower levels sometimes filtered through the bays. Holding as still as possible, not even turning her head, Dani slowed her breathing, taking long, slow draws minimizing any sound or air movement as much as possible. There weren't many vampire Agents; Dani didn't care for any of them but knew their predatory senses were exemplary. She also knew vampires thought that anything not vampire, was prey. Their arrogance, combined with their distain of working with any creature below their perceived status, landed them on most other Agents' "avoid" list.

Would they head to the lower levels or to the garages? The night was still young in the blood eater's world.

"I smell T's funk. Hope we don't see him. I have a hard time not killing the bastard," growled one.

The other male snorted. "I wouldn't even drain him, just take his head off."

"Truth. I drained one of the enhanced Agents once. Never again. I had the shits for a week." Both males laughed as they walked out the door to the hallway, leaving Dani alone once again.

She kept breathing at her slow, steady rate for several more seconds to make sure they didn't come back to investigate. After a suitable amount of time, she straightened and headed straight to the garage entrance.

Agent T's finger worked once again to let her into the garages. She picked out Agent T's 'Stang. He was obsessed with his precious car, trolled for women with it, and spent much of his time off duty buffing and polishing it. A character trait that used to annoy her to no end, she was now completely grateful for otherwise she'd never know what he drove or where it was parked.

Trotting up to the car, anxious to get on the road, her nerves getting the best of her, she dug the keys out of her pocket. Climbing in and inserting the key, the sleek beauty fired up and settled down into a steady purr someone in some other situation would appreciate. But not her, she needed to get going. All the vehicles were parked so they were ready to drive out. And that's just what she did, marginally avoiding squealing the tires.

Hitting the controls to open the double-wide garage door, she steadily increased speed. The door was almost to the top when the security lights against the walls flashed, sirens filling the air. They found her! The door hesitated and began to lower. Dani punched the gas, the engine roared and the car shot forward. Narrowly missing the parked cars, she raced to beat the door. No matter what, she couldn't stop now.

The door kept lowering, sirens blared, red and blue lights lit up the walls as she flew closer to freedom. Sailing through the door, she ducked her head, as if that would help the car sneak under. Metal screeched, the Mustang jerked but pulled free.

Dani maneuvered the sports car swiftly through the drive, heading to the road. A handful of men and women filtered out of the compound's main entrance, weapons drawn, not knowing who or what their target was. At this point, they didn't know Agent T wasn't driving his car.

Could this really work? Rising hopes were dashed as a rumble of thunder shook the ground. Madame G was into some freaky shit beyond the vampires and shifters that had become a normal part of her life in the last few years. Just what other paranormal hoodoo was out there Dani didn't know. And she wasn't hanging around to find out.

Finally, on a straight stretch of road, Dani floored it. Lightning whipped around her. A crack of thunder rattled the windows, a streak of blinding light flashed across the hood, hitting a large tree next to the road just ahead of her. The tree trunk blew out, sending splinters raining down on the roof as she flew by. Another flash even farther ahead struck a tree at a narrower, weaker spot. Dani watched as if in slow motion the top two-thirds of the tree falling to block the road. Dani swerved as far she could, riding the ditch, almost losing control as large branches and leaves temporarily blocked her view. It sounded as if a thousand keys were scratching the paint, each in a different direction. If Agent T could indeed be brought back from the dead, this would do the trick. Triumphant, the Mustang cruised through the debris, missing the main part of the trunk.

Dani let out a whoop and eased back onto the main part of the gravel road. She was smart enough to not go balls out, but pushed the speed as much as she could before she risked losing too much control on the loose surface. They would be following her, there was no doubt. Madame G, in her haste, created an obstacle with the tree that would only delay her pursuers.

Dani screamed as a dark shadow landed on the hood. Fishtailing, she frantically tried to gain control. A sinister, pale face bared fangs through the windshield. The vampire pulled his arm back to smash the glass. His strength would be enough to shatter the glass and pull her through. If he got a hold of her, it was over.

She slammed on the brakes, risking more fishtailing. Agent What's-His-Letter flew off, stunned. As she slammed on the gas again, she punched the window control lowering the glass, and pulled her gun loose. Speeding forward, she aimed for the body that was righting itself in the middle of the road.

Grateful for Agent X and Agent E and their thorough training with sidearms, she held the gun out the window with her left hand and fired off a shot. The male snarled at her, spun around and crouched, preparing to attack the car again. She hit him square on, his body flinging backward. The car shook and heaved when it ran over the rolling vampire in the middle of the road.

Outrunning Madame G's unnatural storm and the dark form in the middle of the road, Dani didn't slow a bit. The vampire was only stunned and would continue his attack if she was close enough. They couldn't fly like birds, but with their super speed, he could catch up and land on a moving target. She was almost to the paved main road and if she could make it there, not even vampire speed would be enough.

Slowing only slightly, Dani turned onto the main road, almost losing control but recovered quickly. Glancing down the gravel road she had just turned off of, she could see headlights. They were after her. Sigma favored dark sedans and SUVs; sedans were inconspicuous and the bigger vehicles could get deep into the woods to dump bodies, and dark colors didn't show bloodstains as badly. But they wouldn't be as fast as her ride. Agent T and his sports car fetish were an asset to her freedom.

Praying she would pass no cops tonight, Dani traversed the desolate back roads to Freemont. The headlights behind her stayed in the distance as she reached the outskirts of town. Slowing only to prevent an accident, Dani sped through the city heading south, aiming for the last bridge crossing the river that separated Freemont from West Creek. Pale Moonlight was on the outskirts of town and was the most likely place she'd find shifters. The most likely place she'd find Guardians. X was right, they would fiercely protect their young—if she could convince them she carried one. Madame G wasn't omnipotent, but no one knew the bounds of her powers or the well she drew them from. Dani only knew the storm she had seen tonight, the one that *attacked* her, was a helluva feat and she could only guess what dark entity Madame G sold her soul to for those powers.

No one had caught up to her as she crossed the river and maneuvered through West Creek. It wasn't as large and sprawling as the city she'd just left, but Dani wasn't as familiar with the layout. Her last three years were spent mostly on the road, returning to Sigma's Freemont compound only to regroup and restock ammo before taking off again. That wasn't the norm for most recruits. They were utilized in the field for the more foolhardy missions, but those showing potential were groomed and trained.

Not Dani. Part of her deal when she signed on was hunting the males that destroyed her life. Killing her family in front of her eyes, laughing as they'd tried to run from the feral shifters. They'd gunned her dad down and were chasing Dani and her mother when distant sirens signaled help was on the way. Showing no mercy, intending to leave no witnesses, they decided to shoot the women and be gone before help arrived. During the shower of bullets, Dani's mom had thrown herself over her daughter, saving her from the life-ending barrage.

When the police arrived, they found Dani pinned under her mother's limp body, bleeding from superficial wounds. Her mom had taken the bullets meant for both of them, saving her child like a mother was supposed to do. Like Dani was doing tonight. She felt the life inside of her and needed no pink line to tell her she was pregnant. Madame G made the mistake of thinking that a shifter's young would gladly be turned over when the due date was up. This baby was all hers, regardless of paternity. And like the young's grandmother, Dani was prepared to die protecting it. Refuge with the Guardians was the first step, then they would need to figure out what Madame G had invested in this child and if she had doctored the sperm sample before inseminating Dani.

The club's sign came into view. Dani needed to think about the rest of her plan. It had originally been to get to Pale Moonlight, find a shifter, and demand to see the Guardians. They had to be there. She heard stories of The Den. A hot streak of anger shot through her. What if she found the Guardians, *her Guardian*, and he was doing exactly what he'd done with Janice? Pounding began in her ears, the anger morphing to rage. What was this? She'd never even met the father of her baby—didn't know what he looked like, but the thought of him touching another female incited her to homicidal levels. She was only weeks into her pregnancy, how was she going to last months?

First, she had to survive tonight. The club was still going strong, the door opened and two forms wandered out, looking down the road in her direction. Damn. Of course they had spies on the shifters, and those spies were notified about the recruit in the red Mustang needing apprehending. She should've jacked another car in Freemont.

Hitting the gas she flew past the club. The Guardian headquarters was supposed to be south of town. Maybe her mediocre lucky streak would continue and she would come across them while outrunning the men that had just jumped into a dark sedan and were in pursuit.

The passenger side mirror blew out. Metal pinged once, twice. They were shooting at her. Dani ducked as low as she could and still drive. Must have been aiming at the tires. They'd face a punishment worse than death if they killed her. But at these speeds, a blown out tire *could* kill her.

The Mustang flew farther away from town with the men close behind. Dani didn't dare turn onto any side roads, didn't dare risk losing control on the gravel roads, didn't dare risk slowing down

A pop and more fishtailing had her slamming on the brakes. They'd gotten a tire. If she could stop this thing without killing herself, maybe she could take them. She'd never been in the field alone before, but most Sigma Agents just saw her as a recruit, forgetting she had three years of field training by two of the best Agents under Madame G. Most recruits didn't really know her at all. She didn't know these men chasing her, but they didn't know her, either, and she could use that to her advantage.

The car skidded around before screeching to a halt on the deserted blacktop. No other cars were in sight, just her and the dark sedan she was now facing. They came to a stop pretty close to her and were getting out, weapons drawn, shouting orders.

Opening the door and climbing out Dani kept her right arm hanging limp facing away from the men, like it was injured. Their headlights shone in her eyes and she held her other hand up. Time to play helpless female.

"You—you gotta help me!" she stuttered.

"Stop! Put your hands up," one of the men ordered.

Almost clear of the hood of her car, she had only seconds before she needed to act. The men were both coming around the protection of their respective car doors, giving her a good shot. Whipping her right hand up and taking aim, she dropped the man closest to her with a head shot and turned on the other who shouted in outrage and charged her, knocking the gun out of her hand before she squeezed off a second shot.

He pushed her back onto the hood, wrestling with her. They would've rolled off onto the ground, but the vampire had left a nice dent that Dani was stuck in. She couldn't get a good purchase on anything, her feet dangling above the ground. Her attacker was trying to get her wrists together to cuff her. She fought like an animal, snarling and biting anything that came close to her mouth, using her legs in any way possible to kick and squirm, but her strength was failing fast against her larger opponent. He probably hadn't been sick in bed for the last two weeks.

A large black shadow crossed her vision, lifting the weight of the man she'd been struggling against with it. She was jerked forward since he still had hold of her wrists, but broke free quickly and rolled off the side of the hood. Peeking over the front of the car, she took in the scene before her.

In an eerie almost complete silence, a large black wolf with streaks of silver gleaming over the fur in the headlights, quickly dispatched the man who had been subduing her only seconds before. The only sounds were grunts and gurgles, until the man's movements ceased altogether. The wolf lifted his head from the man's neck and swung to face her, mouth drawn up in a snarl, blood dripping from his fangs.

Dani was entranced. Each small movement the wolf made, sent ripples of silver through the dark fur. His snout lifted, sniffing the air. The eyes that watched her gleamed with predatory reflection, flashing the same shade of dark silver that rippled through the fur.

Father.

The word whispered through her mind. Her baby was only a bundle of cells. X said some expectant mothers, *shifter* mothers, felt a mental connection with the child they carried. She was human and only in the earliest stages of pregnancy. Did Madame G do something to either of them to create a bond this strong?

A low growl rumbled through his body as she rose to standing. On four legs, he was taller than waist height, and thick in the shoulders and chest. Shifters were larger than standard wolves, Guardians even bigger. He was gigantic.

"Are you the one they call Mercury?"

No longer snarling, he tilted his head to the side and closed his eyes as if letting her voice wash over him. He opened his eyes, the pools of silver regarding her carefully. She watched in fascination as rich, dark fur transformed to smooth skin in front of her eyes.

Her eyes wide, she followed his form as he stood to his full height. Taller than her by a good eight inches, he wasn't as tall as she heard most Guardians were. At probably six-one or two, any perceived lack of height was made up for in width. Wide muscular shoulders were set on top an equally wide and well-defined chest and back, tapering down with rippling abs into heavily-muscled legs. He was also completely naked. Not being an admirer of naked man parts, she had to admit, his size was impressive… all over.

Forcing herself to look into his eyes, she was mesmerized. They hadn't changed as he transformed into his human form, gleaming silver in the dark depths. His hair was dark like his wolf's fur had been, his strong, square jaw clenched. Nostrils flared, he was still scenting the air.

She licked her suddenly dry lips, the movement capturing his complete attention. Her only hope was with the Guardians. Their headquarters wasn't top secret, but she heard no one had been able to enter it since these Guardians set up shop. Sigma could barely *find* it, and only knew the approximate location. But anyone searching for it would get turned around and lost for days. A couple of months ago, she heard four recruits were sent to these woods, loaded for bear—wolves in this case—and were never seen or heard from again.

"Are you Mercury?" she asked again.

"Who the fuck are you and why do you smell like you're carrying my baby?"

Chapter Four

Mercury growled. He couldn't stop it before it rumbled through his chest. The onslaught of emotions and questions stampeded through his mind. He took in the woman before him. Human, there was no doubt. Not enhanced, but what job she held in Sigma he didn't know. He would, however, find out. Her fine-boned, almost regal face had him wondering if she'd led a privileged life. She had full pink lips and long dark brown hair, almost as dark as her eyes. Eyes a guy could get lost in. They held many of her emotions in check, but he could see the flickers of feelings moving deep inside. She was scared, but determined.

The little slip of human squared off in front of him. She smelled of blood (someone else's) and death, but it wasn't hard to get to her scent underneath it all. Womanly and refreshing, she smelled crisp like citrus. Like she should be just as naked as he, lying on a beach, sipping mojitos and soaking up rays.

She also smelled like him. Faint undertones of Mercury laced her scent. That only happened when a woman was with child, with a shifter's child, in this case… his child. That was impossible.

"I *am* carrying your baby," she replied.

"Impossible," he said simply. And it was.

Her eyes took on an accusatory note. "Please, I've heard of you Guardians. Did you not think there were no consequences for playing like you do?"

He raised his eyebrows at her tone. Play? "And you're saying we *played* together?"

She shook her head and nervously looked around. "Redhead, big boobs, couple of months ago? Janice?"

At his blank look she continued, "Madame G sent her in to, ah, harvest from you and inseminate me, somehow thinking I could bear your young. Look, I will gladly tell you everything I know once we get somewhere safe. She wants me back, bad. They'll find me."

He stood, in all his bare glory, regarding her silently. She was edgy, shifting from foot to foot, glancing repeatedly down the highway with dread anticipation.

Finally, he spoke, "Why do you smell like a dead Agent?"

"Cuz I had to kill one to get out of there," she said matter-of-factly.

"Are you an Agent?"

"No."

"Recruit?"

"No. I told you. Somehow, Madame G knew I could get pregnant by you and kept me captive until she had what she needed from you."

She looked down the road again and he smelled her fear. Risking a quick glance himself, he saw headlights in the distance. Quickly deliberating, it might indeed be Sigma, he decided he needed to find out the truth so she had to come with him.

"Get in the car," he nodded to the Agents' car still idling in the middle of the lane. "I'll load them up, then I'll drive."

Relief flooded her eyes and she turned to follow his directions.

"Wait," he ordered her. "Raise your arms, I'm taking your weapons."

"But…" she sputtered, but said no more and raised her arms.

Mercury moved up behind her, her back ramrod straight. Normally, he'd frisk her and be done. But he felt the need to warn her. "I'm going to pat you down."

With her terse nod, he began. Moving as quickly and efficiently as he could although it was hard to ignore the body under his hands. He felt hard muscles and womanly curves under the clothes he patted. Gruffly, he asked her to remove the knives she had hidden on her body. Again, normally he'd just take them—didn't matter if it was a male or female he dealt with. Both genders had tried killing him. But this female… If what she said was true, life would've been pretty traumatic for her with Sigma. And if she was telling the truth, she carried his young.

The scent teased his nostrils. She smelled of rank blood. He found the cloth in her pocket along with the finger, but it must coat her, too. Death lingered around them. The Agent she took out and the one he'd killed enveloped them with fragrance, but her scent was the one that teased his nose. Wafting to him, laced with the subtle scent of his essence that wasn't possible unless he was becoming a dad. Him being a father should be impossible, but what she was saying… plausible. But how? And that feeling someone, somewhere, needed him had abated as soon as he spotted her. His midnight need to run, and changing his route midflight to this highway, he found her fighting for her life. More than coincidence.

Once she'd unloaded her stash from her body, there was a nice little pile of gear sitting on the pavement next to his bare feet.

"Go on, get in," he ordered, not wanting her to hear how much she affected him. Her scent was threatening to drive him mad, and her fierce beauty and the pat down threatened to put on display exactly how much. Okay, it was too late.

"I'll load up the bodies." That should put a dent in his erection. "You got anything you need in the other car?"

She shook her head as she stepped around the agent she had dropped with a head shot. "It belonged to the Agent I killed. I didn't have time to grab anything but…" She gestured to the little pile of guns and knives.

While she climbed in, he hauled both bodies to the back by the trunk. She jerked when he leaned into the driver's side to hit the trunk latch. Her eyes flickered to him and flicked away just as quickly. He was still nude, but there was nothing he could do about that until they got back to the lodge. Once the bodies and weapons were loaded, he again leaned in and ripped out the car's GPS and threw it into the Mustang. It was the most obvious way Sigma could track the vehicle. They would dump it later, probably on Sigma's doorstep with a note that said something witty Bennett made up, like "I swear they were dead when we got here."

When he slid into the driver's seat, she stiffened again.

"What's your name?" he asked, as he guided the car around the stalled Mustang. The headlights were closing in. They wouldn't need to backtrack, he could get to the lodge using roads further down.

"Dani." She spoke quietly, but her voice was strong. She kept glancing in the mirror, gauging how close the other car was.

"Dani what?"

She paused, obviously deciding what or how much she told him. Or maybe even whether to tell him the truth or not.

"Daniella Maria-Sofia Santini."

Shiiiit. Her name caressed its way through him. His cock twitched again. The way it rolled off her tongue, with a slight hint of accent, like she was born American, but grew up with another language spoken around her. Italian? Maybe she was bilingual.

"And you?" she asked. "Mercury what?"

"Just Mercury. You don't look Italian."

She glanced at him, eyebrow arched. "What's Italian supposed to look like?"

"Jersey Shore."

Her mouth quirked at the idea of him watching reality shows. "Only my dad was full Italian, his parents were from the old country. My mom's ancestry was mostly northern European. And I'm not from Jersey."

They drove in silence. Mercury turned off the main highway, traversing back roads, dirt paths, and roads that were often little more than trails, until they reached the lodge. He studied her reaction to their headquarters. She seemed genuinely impressed, not smugly triumphant like she found a way to their home and couldn't wait to get the information back to Sigma.

He wanted her to like it and tried to see it as a newcomer might. A human. Moonlight filtered through the trees but it would be hard for her to make out detail with the shadows. Their cabins, interspersed through the trees, could not be seen at night as they blended too well. The lodge stood tall and dark, moonlight reflections gleaming off the large front windows. The rest of the building became one with the darkness.

He pulled up close to the door. "Wait here."

Dani was studying the building, trying to make out details in the dark, but she made no move to get out.

Mercury got out and let out a howl, sensing Dani jump inside the car. Dani. The nickname suited her. Tough, but feminine. He went around and opened her door. By the time she got out, dark shapes were coming out of the trees from around the lodge.

She stiffened when she noticed the movement. Mercury stood behind her.

"Mercury, are you bringing home strays?" Bennett called.

As they closed in, Mercury could see they were all dressed for battle. He wanted to step in front of Dani, protect her from scrutiny and malice. These were his people, Guardians he trusted with more than his life, he should feel protective toward them instead. He resisted the urge, staying where he was.

"Mercury?" Commander Fitzsimmons questioned. Their leader was a male of few words, but he conveyed much with his tone.

Mercury sensed Kaitlyn and Jace in the trees, listening intently, but ready to provide extra support if needed. It seemed laughable, this little slip of a woman had five Guardians at the ready, but he had the feeling it wouldn't be enough for the drama she brought to their door.

He knew exactly when Bennett and the commander caught the scent that had been haunting Mercury.

"What the…" Bennett trailed off.

"She says she's carrying my young."

"Impossible." Bennett repeated Mercury's first thought.

Dani stood completely still, her eyes shifting from the commander to Bennett. He sensed her resolve, her determination, but her fear almost overwhelmed both. Commander Fitzsimmons studied her with meticulous intensity, Bennett with abject disbelief.

"She said Madame G knew she could bear my young."

Bennett scoffed.

"And how would she know that?" Commander Fitzsimmons quietly spoke to Dani. Her fear spiked another notch, but she just shrugged a little.

Bennett rolled his eyes. "How would Madame G know some random human could carry one of our young?"

"She's not random. She's my mate."

Stunned silence followed Mercury's declaration. Dani felt the blood drain from her face. This was a bad idea. Really bad. *Mate?* The behemoth of a male would never let her go now. She came seeking protection for her baby, not realizing she'd entertained the notion that someday she and the child could escape. Odds just dropped drastically. She'd worry about that later. Right now, she had to secure protection. Madame G could not get her hands on this child.

The males fell silent, eyes snapping between her and Mercury. Both males were tall, taller than Mercury but not as wide, though heavily muscled themselves. And dressed, thank goodness. The stunning blond looked almost horrified at Mercury's declaration that he had a mate, she was it, and she was pregnant. Their leader remained impassive, no doubt taking in all the information and deciding what to do with her.

"Take her to Interrogation Two. We'll talk with her after you get dressed."

Nerves were going to get the best of Dani soon. It had been a long day and even more trying night, followed by a tense car ride with a very naked shifter male. A Guardian male. The father of the life that grew inside of her. Immense relief flooded her by being with him, but she couldn't explain it. Sigma had felt wrong for so long, but being here, surrounded by wary males who didn't trust her, perhaps never would—especially if they found out her true story, felt more right than anything she'd done in years, even after she'd hunted their kind, seeking to satisfy a vengeance born one fateful night years ago.

The tall blond led the way into the massive log building. Dani couldn't make out much in the dark, there were no porch lights, just moonlight.

There was no need as the males could see perfectly well in the dark. Inside, nothing was lit and the shifters were completely silent, leading her down a pitch black hallway.

She experienced a small moment of panic when she sensed Mercury's absence from behind her. He'd said nothing since his mate declaration. As quickly as he was gone, he was back with a slight rustling of material. Clothes. It would be a shame to cover his magnificent body with its bronzed skin rippling over loads of muscle, but a welcome shame as his nudity unnerved her. She spent the time in the car searching out the window to see if they were being followed, but it served double duty to keep her eyes off Mercury's handsome looks, impressive physique, and large package. Otherwise her mind might have wandered to what conceiving naturally by him would've been like, to have his broad back covering her and those rounded, heavily muscled thighs between hers.

Wrong time, wrong place, wrong mental image. These guys could kill her. They wouldn't. She knew it instinctively. Torture maybe, if they felt she was a threat to them. She wouldn't give them any reason to think so. She'd give them most of the truth, lying only by omission. Omission of a few key details.

The blond opened a solid door and stood aside for Dani to enter first. Light slowly began illuminating the room, allowing her vision to adjust without the assault of instant blinding light, which she would have tolerated better than those who surrounded her. Humans didn't have many sensory advantages over these creatures, but it was nice to have at least one.

"Have a seat," the blond's low voice rumbled. If memory of gossip was correct, this one was Mercury's partner. He was the congenial playboy who offset Mercury's quiet, on and off the field. She'd heard impressive tales of both of them and she didn't want to think about them at this time.

Pulling a metal chair back, she sat down. Waves of exhaustion flowed through her as the long adrenaline rush since waking up to Agent T began to dissipate. Her head spun, nausea threatening to upset her already empty stomach.

"What's wrong?" Mercury asked. He was dressed in a black t-shirt which was stretched across his broad shoulders, barely circling his bulging biceps, along with black sweat pants and bare feet.

"I just haven't been feeling well and tonight's catching up to me." Did she look as bad as she felt that he picked up on her feeling ill?

None of the males moved.

"Would a little food help? Water?" Mercury retained his wariness, but seemed attuned to her needs.

"Yes, please."

None of the males moved.

"Bennett. Get some crackers or something." Mercury didn't look to his partner, keeping his scrutiny on Dani.

"We're not a fucking bed and breakfast. We're here to question her, Merc."

"She can't answer if she's throwing up and I'm not leaving this room." Mercury pinned Bennett with his dark eyes, silver swirling in their depths.

"Go ahead, Bennett," the third Guardian ordered. He must be Commander Fitzsimmons, Agent X's nemesis. Dani could have guessed who he was even if he didn't speak. He carried a heavy air of authority along with the obvious respect of the others.

Bennett's navy-blue eyes flashed with irritation, but he left to grab her some food.

"How far along are you?" the commander asked, directing his keen hazel eyes toward her. Dani suppressed the urge to squirm. Being in the room with these shifters was unnerving at best, but now the interrogation would start and they would study her tone, note any hesitation, any fidgeting, anything that would hint she was lying.

Mercury's eyes met hers when she glanced at him.

"Only a couple of weeks."

"What's your name?"

"Dani."

"Your full name."

She gave it to them, there was no reason not to. They would look for information on her and they'd find it. They'd learn about her mom and dad, and the night that changed her life and brought her to this table. Nothing more after that.

"Italian?"

"Somewhat."

Bennett came back into the room, setting a glass of water and a bag of oyster crackers in front of her. "It's all I could find. We aren't much for crackers around here."

Dani muttered, "Thanks." Then dubiously eyed the water glass while she opened the crackers.

"So, tell us," Bennett said, "why would you think you're pregnant with Mercury's baby?"

Chewing slowly, Dani formulated her answer. She didn't need to lie about this, just needed to finish chewing. She was extremely thirsty, especially after dry crackers, and the water taunted her. She'd be damned if she drank it though.

"His scent is on me because it's his baby. I can feel it."

"You ever met her before Mercury?" Bennett asked, clearly not believing her.

Never taking his eyes off her, Mercury solemnly shook his head.

Irritation rose. They hadn't been strapped down and defiled like she was. Their bodies weren't being used as someone's own personal incubator. It wasn't like Janice had to work hard on Mission Semen while they were out doing what they were known for doing besides fighting.

"And you can remember all the girls you've been with? Do you get names and numbers? Take them on second dates?"

"I'd remember you," Mercury said simply, then turned to Bennett. "She said they stole from me and inseminated her."

"Riiight." Bennett leaned back, crossing his arms over his broad chest.

Commander Fitzsimmons' only movement was to narrow his eyes. "How?"

Dani shrugged. "Janice said she got it one night at The Den. That's all I know."

"Janice was an Agent?" Bennett asked.

Dani put her fingers up to make air quotes. "Seduction trainer."

"Where can we find this Janice?"

This time Dani shifted uncomfortably before she stopped herself. Lie by omission. "In the morgue at Sigma. When she found out my insemination was successful she started talking about going back to the club. You guys left quite an impression." She said that a bit more caustically than intended. "They couldn't let her take the chance."

"When was this?" Bennett asked.

"Yesterday."

"No, when was she with us?"

"A couple of months ago."

Mercury and Bennett exchanged looks and each nodded once to the commander.

"Why did Madame G choose you?" the commander continued questioning her.

Dani shrugged. "All she said was she had a good feeling about me. I don't know how."

"Are you enhanced?"

Dani shook her head. "No, I always wondered why she didn't test on me. I think she was afraid if she tampered with me, her plans wouldn't work."

"Are you an Agent?"

She shook her head again.

"Then why were you with them?"

Hesitating long enough to choose her words, she gave a quick run-down of her story. Simplest was best.

"She found me after my parents were killed. Held me prisoner for a few years until she figured out what to do with me. A couple of weeks ago she said I was ready and…" Dani drifted off, struggling to not remember that vile-tasting wine, Agent T's slimy touch…

"And what, Dani?" Mercury spoke low, a faint rumble could be heard emanating from his direction. It was as if he could fill in the blanks and was not happy. That was crazy. He just met her, didn't trust her, and other than the strange bond between them, most likely from the baby, he should feel ambiguous toward her.

Licking her lips, her already dry mouth now parched, she stared at the glass of water.

"Drink first," Mercury urged. "Then finish telling us what happened."

"Do you have bottled water?"

Bennett scoffed, "No, princess."

Mercury scowled at his partner, reached over and took a drink from the glass. "Now drink."

Dani still debated. She was confident they wouldn't poison her, but Madame G was such a fan of administering drugs, Dani became accustomed to not consuming anything she didn't open. Not that it did her any good in the end. Making up her mind, she drained the glass in one long swallow.

Pushing the empty glass to the edge of the table, Mercury looked expectantly at Bennett.

"You don't seriously expect me to go get more?" Bennett's astounded, and slightly offended, tone spoke volumes. Bennett must be the lead in their little friendship, the one who called the shots, and here he was relegated to servant for a woman they'd all just met who hailed straight from the enemy.

Commander Fitzsimmons cut off any more bickering. "We'll get her more after she finishes telling us what she spent her time doing as a prisoner and how she got pregnant."

His hard edge made it obvious he didn't entirely believe her story. She didn't expect them to. Not at first. Maybe with time. Much of it was true, really. She just left out the part where she willingly tracked and killed their species. For Sigma. It didn't matter how evil the creatures were she hunted down, she didn't think the Guardians would be so accepting and offer protection if they knew she had the skills to kill any one of them.

"I was put on menial details. Cleaning and stuff, stayed out of the Agents' way. Then Madame G called me to her floor." Dani took a deep cleansing breath. She could get through this as long as she remembered she gave the bastard what he deserved. "She made me drink wine that had a fertility booster and passed me off to an Agent to…"

Another deep breath and she rushed through the rest. "She told him to have fun with me, but nothing more to avoid contamination. He threw me on the table, stripped me down, but the wine mostly knocked me out. He couldn't have the fun he planned to I guess, so he did what he had to and threw me back in my room." There, that part was done.

"They brought me up for testing each week," Dani continued, the rest was easier and would help them buy her escape story. "But I knew when I was pregnant. So yesterday, when the test came up positive, I had to escape as soon as possible before they monitored me too closely or I got too big to run."

"How'd a little thing like you get away from Madame G if she didn't let you go?" This time scorn was heavy in Bennett's voice.

Mercury sat riveted to her story, not taking his eyes off her. "Who was the Agent?" he growled.

"Agent T. He came back to finish what was started, waiting until he heard the news so he wouldn't get blamed for any negative results. But I had snuck a knife under my pillow a long time ago. For just that reason. I got him across the throat and seized the opportunity."

The low rumbling she heard stopped when she admitted to taking down the Agent. The Guardians continued to study her.

"And in all your time there, you never tried to escape otherwise?" Commander Fitzsimmons asked, disbelief of her story lacing his words.

"I had nothing to go back to. My parents had just been slaughtered. In front of me. And Sigma would've been hunting me."

"Was Sigma involved in the attack?"

Dani wondered the same a few times, but eventually ruled it out. "No, it was an organized hit. My dad was a judge."

The police ruled it as that—her dad was Italian, they lived on the East Coast, it made perfect sense. Dani knew better, but the truth wouldn't be believed. That's why she showed up on Sigma's doorstep when she learned of their mission to wipe out, or control, all shifters.

"So you killed a full-fledged Agent, you're only a couple of weeks pregnant, and you want our help? For how long?" The slight hint of facetiousness in what Commander Fitzsimmons just asked pissed Dani off. She was sick to her stomach, tired, still had dried blood on her, and her boobs hurt, dammit.

"I don't want your help at all," she bit out. "But I *need* it. Do you think I wanted this? Do you think I sat at Sigma's headquarters wishing I could be a Guardian's mate and carry his child? Because one, motherhood was the last thing I was ready for. And two, I really didn't picture myself settling down in the boonies with a man-whore, fearing for my life and my baby's."

Confusion curtained Mercury's devastatingly handsome face. "Man-whore?"

Dani rolled her eyes. "Please. If I literally had any other place to go, *at all*, I would be heading there. Believe me, don't believe me, whatever. Either help me or let me keep going before they totally surround the place."

"Well, well, well." Bennett's lip curled in smugness. "Now our true feelings are showing. You know we can't let you go, a human who knows about us. And they need to find the place before they can surround it. Should we keep her in the holding cell, Boss? Until we figure out what to do with her?" Bennett clearly didn't believe her, but Dani was dismayed to find out how relieved she was when he informed her they wouldn't let her go.

"She'll stay in my cabin," Mercury said abruptly.

"Merc—" Bennett started.

"Not a good idea," the commander interjected.

Dani was even opening her mouth to argue, her heart racing at the thought of being imprisoned in his home, sleeping in his bed. The holding cell sounded just fine. There she could get sleep. Not surrounded by the unusual male's stuff, wondering what made him tick.

Mercury's eyes, gleaming more silver now than when they had all walked into the room, gave one shake of his head, cutting both males off.

"She can have the cabin, I'll sleep on the porch."

"And what if she's a Sigma plant and tries to kill you?"

Mercury pinned her with his intense dark stare. She could get lost in those eyes, hypnotized.

"She won't." Mercury's statement was almost a question, making Dani nod her head in agreement. She truly didn't plan to hurt anyone anymore, Guardian or otherwise. Since the beginnings of life snaked through her, making her aware and extremely protective of it, her only concern had been the safety of that life.

"She's my mate. I will deal with her."

Dani mentally sighed at the last statement. Just what every woman wanted to hear.

"We don't know that Madame G didn't tamper with her or even the baby. We don't know what she is. Stay with her," the commander ordered as he stood up. "Don't let her go anywhere around here by herself, and don't let her leave."

Tearing her gaze off Mercury before she sunk into the depths of that mesmerizing silver-tinted darkness, she saw that the commander was pointedly looking at her. Great. Well, at least they hadn't killed her immediately, and didn't seem to plan to in the near future. Their heightened senses told them what she already knew and felt, that her baby was also Mercury's.

As for the mate business, she wasn't going to think about that. It didn't matter. She wasn't Mercury's mate. Aside from him being a shifter, she wouldn't tie herself to a Guardian with their legendary exploits of violence and women. No matter how much he made her aware she was a woman. Maybe it was the pregnancy amping up her hormones, maybe the waning adrenaline high, but her attraction to him was superficial. He was a stunning creature and she had seen every inch of him.

But how many other women could say that? That thought cooled any curls of desire snaking through her, replacing it with what could *not* be jealousy. She'd just met the guy. Didn't matter, she wasn't his mate.

Bennett was eyeballing her like she was a rattlesnake, ready to strike. The commander had already left the room. Mercury rose in a fluid motion. For a big man, he moved gracefully and silently.

"Come with me, Dani. You can shower and rest at my place."

Chapter Five

The look on his mate's face told Mercury she wasn't comforted at all by the idea of staying at his cabin.

Human. His mate was human. Mercury didn't care. She already knew all about their world and with human mates, that was over half the battle. He also knew Madame G didn't have a hand in this. Dani was his. The baby was his.

Of course, Madame G was involved in more than just orchestrating the events that brought Dani to him. The Guardians would find out how and remove her influence, somehow.

Bennett headed out the door, Dani turned to follow, weaving slightly. Mercury was there to steady her with a hand on her back. That brief touch, even through her shirt, sent a shock up his arm, straight down to his groin.

"I'm fine," she snapped at him, and he jerked his hand back.

Even worn and pale from tonight, she was a beauty. Her dark brown eyes, so expressive, flashing with irritation. Mercury frowned when he remembered her irritation had been at him and the stories she heard about him. Many of them were true. But many were not and he'd discern what needed clearing up and what didn't. Man-whore?

In single file, Dani buffered between the two much larger males, they made their way out into the night. Mercury kept his guard up, he would be a fool to trust someone with such strong ties to Sigma. Her ass, though. He watched it sway in her tight-fitting black pants. She had a lean athletic build, subtle muscles rounding her arms and legs in all the right places, including that ass. Assurance and determination in each step suggested her story of being imprisoned for three years may not be entirely accurate. Big shock. She didn't have the walk of someone who'd spent her time bent over toilets, scrubbing floors, fearing for her life.

They left through the back door, heading deeper into the countryside. This was Mercury's favorite view. Tall, healthy trees, finally filled out after the long winter, nearly hiding the cabins that lay within. Rustic, but sturdy, dwellings littered the acres behind the lodge. With peaked roofs and log sides, the two bedroom cottages that were the living quarters of the individual Guardians didn't look like anything more than quaint little vacation stayovers.

They weren't, though. Well, maybe Mercury's. He wasn't much for tangible goods, preferring action to lounging. Aside from his books, his space was sparsely furnished with minimal, actually no, décor.

When they arrived at Mercury's place, Bennett spoke to him while giving Dani a warning stare.

"You sure about this?"

"Would I have said it if I wasn't?" Mercury got sick of the shadowed talk most people did with each other. He really didn't get the complexities of human interactions. The environment he grew up in, before Master Bellamy brought him into the shifter world to become a Guardian, didn't allow for double meanings. Voiced intentions were followed by actions, otherwise there was no need to speak. Especially since the pack he was raised in with didn't talk—literally.

Bennett continued to give Dani the stink eye and she faced him head-on with her own challenging look. He finally said, "All right then. Howl if you need me."

With Bennett walking in the direction of his living quarters, which was the closest cabin a couple hundred yards away, Mercury took the chance to study Dani. Daniella. What did she prefer?

"What do you want to be called?"

"What?" she asked perplexed, tearing her gaze away from studying Mercury's cabin and the surrounding woods. Her human eyes couldn't make out much in the darkness, but she was taking in what she could.

"Your name. You said it was Dani, but it's Daniella."

"Would I tell you my name was Dani if I hated to be called that?"

Okay.

"Dani fits you, but Daniella's a beautiful name and that fits you, too. It'd be a shame not to use it."

She gave him a wary look. He was used to it, people trying to make out if he was serious, what was the hidden meaning in his words.

She went back to scanning from the cabin to the lodge from where they came. The shadows of the night cloaked her fatigue and paleness, giving her an almost ethereal glow. Her hair was falling out of her ponytail, wisps caressing her face like he couldn't wait to do.

"Only my mom called me Daniella, until Madame G. I hated it coming from her lips."

"And if I were to call you that?"

She spun to face him straight on, hands on her slender hips. He wondered what her belly would look like rounding with his child. His musings were cut short.

"Look, Mercury. Thanks for saving me tonight. Thanks for putting me up. I came to you to protect this baby and that's it. Call me whatever you want." Her words, along with her flat tone, did nothing to answer his question.

Okay. "You can go inside," he inclined his head toward the door.

Lips pursed, she shuffled up the steps. Mercury waited for her to reach the top. That ass, sashaying up the stairs, mesmerized him. Reaching her hand to the door, it swung open before she could touch the knob. A light slowly illuminated the room inside.

"Did you do that?" she asked breathlessly, her shoulders tensed.

"Yeah. Telekinesis is my gift," he answered.

Her shoulders dropped in relief before she hesitated, her brows knit together. Squaring her shoulders again she stepped inside.

He wouldn't tell her his shitty skills at handling telekinesis, for now the less she knew of that the better. She was only a step up from a prisoner, and it was apparent enough that she would not be leading his fan club anytime soon.

"Why do you dislike me? Or is it all shifters in general?"

Her eyes narrowed on him, scrutinizing him.

"You mean, why do I not like finding out I'm supposed to be the mate of one of the biggest womanizing males I've ever heard of? And let's see, how did I find out it was you?" She patted her chin with an index finger. "Hmmm, was it when I heard firsthand how spectacular you were in size and abundance from the most revolting, inhumane woman I've ever met?"

Mercury was at a loss for words against her assault. That's just the way he was, it was always accepted, that's how unmated Guardians acted.

"Oh well," Dani continued, sarcasm dripping from her words, "at least she was legal, cuz I'm sure you had your fair share of underage bait in that club."

Anger was instant and Mercury closed the gap between them, his face inches from hers. Dani clamped her mouth closed and swallowed hard, but didn't back down from him.

"*None*," he bit out from clenched teeth, "of those women were underage. All of them were over twenty-one. *All* of them were willing."

"Willing, but forgettable? Do you even remember Janice? The skank who sucked you dry and took it all back to Sigma?"

Mercury winced at her words and backed off a step. He regretted his outburst. Not what he said, he couldn't let that go untold. Her scent calmed him, snaking in like a summer breeze, soothing his temper. Odd, since she was the one that utterly pissed him off in the first place.

"No. Just from what you said, her timing was one of the last times I blew off steam at the club."

"Well don't let me keep you from 'blowing off steam.'" She gave the last phrase air quotes. "I'm sure you can't go without sex for long and I'm not offering."

"I haven't had sex."

Hands on her hips, she wore a *you're shitting me* look.

"I'm a virgin," he repeated.

Dani snorted. It was the most unfeminine thing she could do and it made her entirely irresistible. He couldn't help but love watching the expressions float across her strong, but delicate features. Even though most of those expressions had been negative and directed at him.

This time he made air quotes. "'Suck me dry' is all I would let them do. The less touching the better. I just needed to get off and I'm sorry if a warm mouth is better than my right hand, but I did that for the first century. And almost half of the next. It's lonely."

He was breathing heavily, not believing he was confessing these details to a woman he just met, especially his mate. He should have known a human mate would have trouble understanding shifters' basest urges. And he should have known the mate he never thought was out there for him might have known about the extra drives and stresses that Guardians face and had heard stories. Fuck, even met some of the participants in those stories. What he didn't expect was the raging jealousy and anxiety coming off Dani in waves. Was this really all about him and his supposedly sordid past?

She'd fallen quiet, but was still pinning him with a hard look.

"Truth be told," he continued in a quieter tone, "it was just as lonely and I've been trying to cope other ways. Just know, there is no one truer than a bonded Guardian."

The hard look had been softening until the last sentence. And it was back. "Well, we're not bonded."

"Not yet."

Dani had the audacity to roll her eyes, but let the topic of conversation drop. The only emotion he could sense from her was extreme fatigue.

"You need to rest. The kitchen is to the left. We'll stock it tomorrow, but there's water. The bed's in that room." Mercury pointed to the right. "You can use anything of mine you need. The gun safe and ammo bin only open for me, so don't bother trying. I'll get my roll and sleep on the porch."

Too tired to argue anymore, Dani nodded numbly and headed toward his room. He followed because he had to get his bedroll off the floor and he wasn't missing another opportunity to see her tightly-clad bottom. Mostly, he felt driven to see her in his room, surrounded by his things, his scent thoroughly encompassing her. He found he could barely wait to see her in the morning after her shower, when the stink of the Agent she killed was off her and he could fill his lungs with who Dani really was.

***

Books. That was his only decoration. Hell, his only possession besides blankets and clothes.

Mercury had rolled up his bedroll—from the floor?—while she stood watching his muscles bunching and flexing, then true to his word, left her alone in the cabin. From there she shuffled into the small, but surprisingly adequate bathroom, then shuffled back out.

What was she going to wear after her shower? Not the blood-tinged shirt and pants that she had carried around a severed finger in. That left naked. No. Or his clothes. Shit. It was practical and he told her to help herself. It just seemed so intimate. Especially after their conversation.

With no other choice, she rifled through his drawers coming up with a black t-shirt that would be like a nightgown on her, and a pair of athletic shorts she could roll down and drawstring to fit. What she didn't find left a slow burn in her belly. No underwear. Made sense, less to remove after shifting and find again later. But knowing he was commando, twenty-four seven, ready for anything, anytime, anywhere…

Gah! Was she a dude now, filled with lust finding out a girl didn't have any panties on? And it didn't matter for guys, whether they wore undies or not, they were always ready anytime, anywhere, and hoped for anything.

Virgin? Dani snorted. Could he really claim that when so many mouths had been closed around him? Jealously threatened to blow her head off. What was going on? Was this the pregnancy emotional roller coaster? It was only related to

Mercury when she couldn't keep her cool, and unfortunately the throat punching was before she even met him.

X called him weird, but seemed to respect the hell out of him as someone she'd come up against. Dani sifted through her mind for any little detail she'd heard over the years as she stripped down and climbed into the bathtub/shower combo still wearing her clothes. She'd rather wash those while she was dirty then have to deal with them later and feel like she needed another shower.

While she worked on scrubbing her duds and her body with the lone bar of soap in the shower, she tried to filter out any specific Guardian from the snippets of gossip passing through the training gym and cafeteria. Sigma had tried to remain under the radar in this location for years while they built up their base and conducted their research. Dani was often out of the area, back where she originated, hunting the rogues who ruined her life, and maybe a couple of others who were real assholes needing to be put down. The Guardians themselves, the police of their species, were busy with their own interspecies issues.

Let's see… she'd heard of the twins. Could've been worse, she shuddered. She could be dealing with future matedom with one of them. Would they share their mate, too? The commander was a formidable male, and she could believe it after meeting the quiet, intimidating Guardian. But not much was known about him other than his field work. He didn't do much that was gossip worthy. Most of the salacious, hushed conversations were about the three who frequented Pale Moonlight, and that was all she heard about them.

The latest she found interesting was that they had added to their pack; a woman, rumored to be Guardian-born, and another male that Sigma had had an unsuccessful mission with. It was uncommon for Guardians to be recruited instead of a member by birthright. But with so many more shifters filtering into the human population, increasing numbers of rogue and feral instances, they probably needed more manpower.

Satisfied she and her belongings were adequate, Dani wrung out her only possessions and strung them up, then reluctantly climbed into Mercury's clothes. As soon as the shirt slid overhead, caressing its way down her sensitive skin, she was enveloped in his scent, like a fresh spring day in the great outdoors.

There were no barriers between her and his items, and like the shifter sleeping on the porch, she was also commando. Agent's shirts usually doubled as their bra support and Dani didn't need a whole lot in that area, always having been a lean girl, and her panties were strung up to dry. At least she could yank them down in the morning, the other items would take longer to dry.

Deciding to get one more drink of water, Dani made her way to the sparse kitchen. Not much different than his bedroom and bathroom, the kitchen contained little, only what was necessary, if that. On the way back to the bedroom, she glanced out the window to see the large sleeping form stretched out on his side in front of the door. His back to the door, his front facing out, ready to take on any danger that might threaten his place. If Mercury knew what filled in the blanks in her backstory, he would be facing the door instead.

Ignoring the anxiety at the when, not if, scenario of the Guardians learning she hadn't been a prisoner, Dani crawled into bed glad she didn't know where the light switch was. They dimmed slightly once she settled under the minimal bedding. Freaky. Mercury must've done that mind magic that his kind could perform. What would it be like to manipulate things with her mind? Recalling the two events from earlier in the evening when her wishes came true, maybe she already had an idea.

Before she could get much farther, sleep claimed her.

**

"Dad!" Dani screamed.

Deep, male laughter that left an evil taint in the air came from the brute to her left. Another thug, with lank, greasy hair and dressed similar, stood to her right. She clutched her mother as they huddled together.

A third male was beating her dad. A constant chime dinged from the family's car door left open when her father had gotten out to check their sudden flat tire. Her dad had been shot in the leg as soon as he stepped out, and while Dani and her mom screamed, they were all dragged onto the road where the women were forced to watch, with terrified incomprehension, as a fanged male with clawed fingers beat her father.

Dani's mother dialed 9-1-1 as soon as they had car trouble in the middle of nowhere. Now Dani just prayed for cell reception and a thorough cop who would decide to follow up on the dropped call.

When her father's body went completely limp, the creature pulled out his gun and pointed it at her dad's head. Seeing the writing on the wall and taking advantage of the other two's rapt fascination with impending death, Dani's mom spun, taking Dani with her, and ducked between the two males.

"Run!" she cried.

And they did. Darting around the car to gain ground from their captors, they flew down the ditch into the surrounding trees. Relief flooded Dani when she heard distant sirens wailing, though they were still a ways off on the desolate highway.

"Kill 'em if we can't play with 'em," one snarled not far behind her.

Bullets hit dirt around her. One male, baring his fangs was fast approaching on her side, his gun, pointed at her torso. He was so close, there was no way he'd miss.

Dani was shoved to the side, her mom turning her body to cover as much of her daughter as she could when the next shot rang out.

Dani was taken down to into the brush with her mother's falling body weight.

"Mom!"

"Fuck! Daniella!"

She came to in the stark, white room. A breeze wafting over her skin. Looking down the length of her naked torso, she found her feet in stirrups, and Agent T between her knees.

"Ow! Shit, Daniella!"

He had her pinned, her wrists manacled in his hand, she couldn't move. His weight was crushing her. Agent T came back to finish what he had started.

"Daniella! Wake up!"

With a gasp, Dani's eyes flew open. Her wrists were caught up in Mercury's hands, his grip already loosening as he gauged her alertness. But he still held on, from the red claw marks on his cheeks, he didn't want to be struck again.

Breathing heavily, Dani glanced around at the unfamiliar surroundings, her panic not yet receding. Soft light filtered in through the windows. She must've gotten some sleep before the nightmares set in. A mountain of muscle rested solidly, but somehow lightly, on top of her. His face was close to hers since he was using the bed to help restrain her flailing arms.

The bewilderment and concern in his swirling, mercury eyes was her undoing. One of those nightmares would torment her all day, but three consecutive?

Her hands flew from his now loosened grip, and she wrapped them around his broad shoulders and buried her face in his neck for solace.

"Are you all right?" he hesitantly asked, cradling her and supporting her weight as she clung to him.

Nodding, she eased back to look at him, strangely comfortable with how close they were, given the fact that she'd kicked off her covers sometime during her slumber. When his head lowered to determine whether she was indeed all right, Dani couldn't resist anymore. She had to know. Would his lips feel as good as they looked?

She met him the rest of the way, claiming his lips. He stiffened, the shock quickly dissipating as he hugged her closer, his knees sliding out so he was stretched out over her, his body a welcome balm for the terror she woke up from.

He was so warm, so solid, and so *real*. She gave her hands free range over his body. When his tongue swept across her lips, she gladly opened them and met it with her own. He explored her mouth like it was the new eighth wonder of the world. The restlessness between her legs throbbed, moisture pooled anticipating his entrance, wanting to be as close to him as possible, to be invaded by his body like her mouth was.

She spread her knees to cradle him between her thighs, he rocked into her. His impressive size stroking her intimately, but relieving nothing. There were too many clothes in the way and he appeared to be in no rush, like he was fascinated with her lips and her tongue, his hands exploring her curves. Once one hand reached her butt, it never left while he used his other hand to slide up her shirt.

A low groan rumbled against her chest as soon as his fingers met her flesh.

"*So soft*," he muttered, against her lips.

Almost desperately pulling up Mercury's black shirt, Dani slid her hands across his chest. Up, gently circling his nipples, smiling when his body shuddered, back down, rimming the top of his sweats. His large size pushed the fabric out of the way, but out of her reach, pinned between their bodies, slowly rocking into her. The thrumming between her legs was torturous, the male above her irresistible, the adrenaline from her nightmare like kerosene. Burning desire was building, demanding release.

Mercury's hand found her breast and cupped it gently, careful but firm. His fingers massaged the nipple.

Heat. Unbearable.

Frustrated, she grabbed his hand from her ass and, thanks to the extra big, extra loose shorts, effortlessly slid it in between them and her body to touch her center.

Abruptly, he stopped their kiss, his forehead on hers in complete awe as he touched her.

"So. Soft," he growled. "So wet."

Rolling her hips into his hand, his fingers threaded between her folds, and she exhaled into him.

It was like she'd gone from zero to one-twenty two seconds after she woke up. His scent, his heat, his emotion, stoked her desire to unheard of levels.

So fast, she should be ashamed if she hadn't needed it so bad, her body peaked and went soaring. Mercury didn't even have to move his hand, she took care of it all with her shudders and spasms as she cried out her orgasm.

The first thing Dani noticed after coming down off the tumultuous waves was that his hand still hadn't moved and she was already moving against it again. The second thing was his heart-wrenching gaze of utter adoration at her, like watching her climax was the most astounding thing he'd ever seen.

The anxiety of when, not if, he found out her secrets threatened to interfere. She couldn't let that happen. She grabbed him up in another kiss to make it go away.

A quick learner, Mercury circled her sensitive bud and tunneled a finger down. Slowly he slide it inside.

"Even wetter," he moaned into her mouth.

Her body clamped down onto him, barely letting him move to slide in and out. She hoped instinct told him to prep her well before trying to fit his massive size into her.

Pounding on the door made them both freeze.

"Mercury! Get some food and meet in the lodge in an hour." Dani recognized Bennett's voice.

To say irritation flashed in Mercury's eyes would be an understatement. Was he growling?

"Merc!"

"Yeah! Fine!" Mercury hollered back.

"Well next time answer your damn texts," Bennett shouted through the door. "Or I'll think the little woman slit your throat in your sleep."

Dani stiffened then forced herself to relax, but Mercury caught the movement and withdrew his finger from inside of her. Her body instantly mourned the loss.

"Leave, Bennett."

"You'd better not be doing her. Dude, you know we can't trust her."

Mercury helped Dani up. "Fuck off, Bennett."

Loud stomps could be heard as Bennett stormed off the porch.

"Sorry. He's, uh—"

"Protective?" Dani finished. Bennett had to know everything about Mercury, and although she had no intention to hurt Mercury—only pleasure came to her mind when she thought of him—she couldn't blame Bennett for looking out for him.

"Yeah. That's it."

"You guys text each other? I thought you all were telepathic or something?"

Mercury's guarded look and considered pause meant he was figuring out what was okay to tell her and just how much. She wasn't fishing for information to use against them, just surprised that paranormal creatures equipped with a variety of mental gifts would be thumbing iPhones to communicate.

"We can be," he finally said. "But it's not working like it should."

Looking at him expectantly, Dani waited for a follow up to his cryptic tidbit.

Instead, he said, "We'd better get ready," and ruffled through the drawers, the huge tenting in front of his sweats had be uncomfortable. Dani shifted, suddenly self-conscious. She was relieved temporarily of the terrible pressure that had been mounting since he popped up naked in front of her last night. It was getting stroked, literally, again when the door pounding scared the ever-loving shit out of her. Mercury took no relief for himself, back to business as usual, but he had to be aching.

When he straightened, his eyes swept her from head to toe, flaring hot. In that instant, her pressure was back, thrumming like it was trying to get closer to the giant male in the room. His gaze traveled her body slowly, like he was remembering how she felt and the sounds she made when his hands worked her.

"I'll change in the other room. You can have the bathroom." Adjusting his sweats, he headed out the door.

Dani briefly recalled another bedroom in the cabin; it was empty. On her way to the bathroom, she stopped to read some of the titles of books on his shelves. She wouldn't have pegged him for a reader. But interestingly, there was quite a variety: classics, contemporary, mysteries, textbooks. The wear and tear on them meant they weren't just for show, he probably even moved around with them.

That thought led her to wonder how old he was. Shifters lived much longer than humans. As his mate, if she bound herself to him, she would share his life span. Even acquire his self-healing abilities. Maybe she should bind herself to him before the stretch marks started.

Holy shit! The hot mess that greeted Dani in the bathroom mirror startled her musings away. The bar soap and lack of conditioner, not to mention the thrashing from the nightmare, gave her long, chocolate hair all kinds of free rein to get tangled up. But under the rat's nest, her dark eyes sparkled and her cheeks retained their flush from being with Mercury. The memory caused her to flush even more and her already taut nipples to poke further through the t-shirt material, so now she looked like a thoroughly sexed-up woman.

Frantically trying to finger comb her hair without ripping it out, Dani got it manageable and tied it back on itself into a loose ponytail. Mercury owned soap, a razor, toothpaste, and a toothbrush. That was it. Those four things, along with the towels, were all the items in the small bathroom.

Sighing, as she checked her clothes to determine if they were at all dry, Dani thought it just wasn't fair he could look as good as he did without an arsenal of supplies. Humidity wasn't bad in West Creek and they were deep in the woods surrounding the town, so at least her underwear was dry. The rest would need more time. Throwing the panties on, she folded and tied the shorts and tied the bottom of the t-shirt so it wouldn't hang too badly on her breasts, announcing how Mercury made her feel.

Waiting patiently at the door, absorbing the sight of her, all he said was, "Ready?"

"I don't have shoes," she said, pointing to her boots from last night sitting by the bed. She could wear them, this wasn't the time to be concerned about fashion, but seriously, boots with her outfit would look atrocious and that bothered her when it shouldn't.

He quirked an eyebrow at the boots, obviously wondering why she wouldn't wear them.

"The path to the lodge isn't too bad and we'll be down there for a while. I'm sure the commander wants to talk with you more. If you don't plan on running, you won't need them." The last sentence was said with a growl underlying the words.

"Let's go, then," she said, almost defiantly. She wanted to run from Mercury and the feelings he stirred in her, and the memory of his touch. Mothers had to protect their young and as long as she was pregnant with a baby who Sigma desperately wanted, she would cling to any protection the Guardians offered.

As long as she was pregnant. It was so early yet. What if she didn't carry to term? She had just graduated college when she joined Sigma. Before she lost her family, one of her older friends had gotten married and became pregnant. Dani recalled her excitedly spilling the news, officially announcing the due date, only to lose the baby shortly after the first trimester.

Concerns and questions, so many questions, were flying around in her head as she followed Mercury down the path to the lodge, picking her way carefully with her bare feet.

"What's wrong?" he asked, abruptly rounding on her. "I can smell your worry."

Damn shifters and their senses. Could he smell her desire, too? Could the others? Would they smell Mercury on her, or figure it was from their close proximity the last twelve hours? She blinked up at him, suddenly aware of the bright sun shining in her face. It was a beautiful summer day and she had no idea what time it was.

"Are you worried about the commander? Meeting the others?" he asked.

"No, actually. I really don't care about spilling on Sigma and any secrets of theirs I might know. I'm just wondering—" It felt suddenly too intimate to talk baby with this man, who was the father. "Nine months is a long time, and it's so early. What if…"

Caught by how painful it was to voice the thought of losing the life forming inside of her, Dani found she couldn't really say it out loud.

Mercury's brows drew together. "What if what?"

Reformulating her words to almost think hypothetically. "Well, you know, some women miscarry."

"Do you feel like something's wrong?"

"What do you mean?"

Mercury shrugged. "Our people are very intuitive, in touch with nature and our bodies. You're human, but our baby," he paused on those words, an unreadable look flitting across his face, "will be a shifter. Look in on yourself and see if you can feel something wrong."

How was she supposed to do that? Closing her eyes, letting the warm sun's rays melt into her, she concentrated on the area in her abdomen where the little one grew.

Chapter Six

It was a breathtaking sight. Dani, with her face turned up into the sun, eyes closed, a half smile almost overtaking the worry he'd scented from her just a moment ago. Her messy ponytail hung down her neck, caressing her delicate skin in place of his tongue.

He'd had a taste of her and wanted more. She'd let him into her body and he wanted deeper. He wanted to explore every inch of her skin, inside and out with his hands, his tongue. He wanted to feel her heat and moisture wrapped around him. Instinctively, he knew he hadn't been missing anything. Kissing and touching wouldn't have felt the same with anyone else. He couldn't stand the thought of other women touching him any more than they had to. He just knew it was something to be saved for his mate. As a Guardian, mates aren't found very easily and his rocky start in life, and difficulty tolerating people, didn't give him much hope of finding his.

Before he sported another massive, painful erection, he decided he'd better do something. She was worried about their baby. Their baby. Would he ever get used to that? He wasn't allowed consent or the pleasure of her body, neither was she, to make this baby. Regardless, a baby was made from them and she was scared.

He concentrated on her lower belly, zeroing in like he had x-ray vision. As she went inward, he went outward.

A warmth spread through his mind, lighting up dark corners he'd given up hope on. A soft gasp came from Dani as if she felt him too, like he was feeling her. Tied to her presence was the tiny kernel of awareness he'd come to associate with his young. A thrill went through him, then a dawning comprehension of dismay.

"Did you feel that?" she asked breathlessly, her eyes glittering excitedly in the sun. "I didn't think it would work, but then I felt you and it was like a booster pack and I swear I could feel it."

Shoving this new information to the back of his mind so he could talk with Commander Fitzsimmons later, he gave her a forced smile.

"We'd better get you some food before we meet the others."

The excitement drained from her face and made him want to growl at himself. She must not have felt what he did. Fucking Sigma.

They entered through the back door of the lodge and wove their way to the kitchen. Another Guardian, Mason, was sitting at the table, scrolling through his tablet, chewing on strips of bacon. The males glared at each other since Mercury could feel the man's distaste of his mate. He sat Dani at the far end so she didn't have to be next to the infuriating male. Mercury rummaged through the cabinets for food. Grabbing the rest of the bacon and slices of toast he sat across from Dani and dished out their food.

Stiffly she chewed her food, sensing the unease between the males, which wouldn't be hard even for a regular human. Mason had been difficult lately, and with a human "visitor" they knew very little of, he anticipated nothing but antagonism from his fellow Guardian.

Kaitlyn breezed into the kitchen. The tall female's coppery red hair was braided down her back and she wore the standard Guardian black shirt and black tech pants.

"Mornin' bitches."

Mason grunted, Mercury muttered his greetings. Slamming doors and cupboards as she ruthlessly searched for her cereal and raided the fridge for milk, Kaitlyn was a force to be reckoned with in everything she did. Plopping down across from Mason, a couple chairs away from Mercury, she smiled over at Dani.

"So, you're Mercury's mate we know nothing about?" Her tone was teasing, not insulting, and Mercury was grateful for her friendlier reception, despite the lack of trust.

"Yeah, Mercury," Mason's tone dripped deviance, a cruel smile lifting his mouth, "why don't you introduce your little human to Kaitlyn?

I'm sure she can fill her in on aaaall about how to please you."

Mercury froze and Dani's hand stilled midway to her mouth.

"Aw, Mason!" Kaitlyn said, her mouth full of half-chewed cereal. "You asshole. You know humans don't understand." Milk dripped down her chin and with typical Kaitlyn elegance, she swiped at it with the back of her hand. Uncouth was a word he'd come to associate with the new Guardian.

"Fuck, Kaitlyn," Mason said, with only a touch of derision and more exasperation. "You eat like a dog."

Chewing on another large spoonful, she remained hunched over her bowl like she was afraid it would get grabbed out from under her nose and flipped Mason off.

She looked at Dani with an apologetic smile. "I tend to forget, but as Mason pointed out, I once got in on the action at Pale Moonlight with your dude and the blond with the stick up his ass." She winked at Dani. "But it was before I knew I could grow fur and it never meant anything. At least to me." She leaned over and slugged Mercury in the shoulder. He let out a little *oomph* and shook his head. Her strength was really coming along. "Maybe this poor bastard can quit pining for me now that you're here."

Trying to gauge Dani's reaction, Mercury studied her while chewing his bacon. She had a sort of dazed and confused appearance, having gone back to eating her own food, watching everything play out. It seemed like she didn't know what to make of Kaitlyn. Mercury could empathize. While he was quite fond—not in *that* sense—of the female, she was an unpredictable, but reliable, force. His empathy also extended to the new Guardian. Watching her trying to understand herself and this new world brought out memories from eons ago when Master Bellamy pulled him from his pack and showed him where he belonged. Only, it took decades to think maybe he did belong, and he often wondered if he hadn't been better off roaming the wild with his pack of natural wolves.

Mason stood, snarling something derogatory about humans while he was turning to go, making sure it was loud enough for her ears.

Mercury flew out of his chair.

"Stop."

That one word uttered from his mate halted him. Mason disappeared, chuckling maliciously.

"I don't give a shit who believes me, who doesn't; who hates humans, who doesn't; who had their face in your crotch, who didn't. I really don't. All I care about right now is this bacon and if there's any more, because I'm starving. 'K?"

Still frozen in his semi-leap position, Mercury was bewildered by her declaration—didn't know what to make of it.

"You heard the lady," Kaitlyn told him. "Get her some damn bacon."

Dani gave her a whisper of a smile and looked expectantly at Mercury.

He was dishing up more bacon fresh from the oven when he sensed Bennett enter the kitchen.

"Kaitlyn, you're with me today. We've got a domestic north of West Creek. Piece of shit keeps beating his mate, turned on his kids." Turning to Mercury, Bennett continued, "Mercury, Boss wants to interrogate the spy."

At the warning growl, Bennett slung him a placating look. "*Dani.*"

All business, Kaitlyn cleaned up her stuff and marched out of the kitchen. Mercury was surprised they were allowing her out in the field since she still passed out after her shifting. Her fighting skills as a human were admirable and would get her by as long as Bennett was there.

Eyes flicking between Mercury and his mate, Bennett watched Mercury serve her.

"Be careful," Bennett warned.

Mercury ignored him and sat back down. Almost as soon as Bennett left, he heard the other two newbies to their pack approaching.

Feminine laughter wafted in ahead of Cassie and Jace's arrival. Jace had a shit-eating grin on his face, gave Mercury a quick nod, and went to gather breakfast for his own mate.

Cassie sat where Kaitlyn had just been, knowing better than to sit next to the woman with the shady past.

"Dani, right?"

"That's right. Apparently, this is the meet and greet." It was a statement, said with no sour notes in her voice.

Cassie laughed gently. "Busted. I'm Cassie. Look, while you're here, you'll need some clothes." She dug into the monster purse most women insisted on carrying around. Cassie also needed hers to conceal a gun and knife since she was also only human. Being bound to Jace came with the usual perks of quicker healing and longevity, but Sigma would not hesitate to snatch and grab her again.

Producing paper and pen, she slid them over to Dani. "Write your sizes and any special requests. We'll get you enough to get by."

"Oh. No. You can't. I mean, I don't have any money or anything to pay you back."

Cassie delivered a reassuring look. "It's all right, it won't be that much. It's not like I'm bringing back designer labels. I get you're not a typical guest, but you can't be running around barefoot, drowning in Mercury's clothes."

Dani still hesitated, obviously uncomfortable with the charity.

"I'm sure we can find a chore for you to earn your keep until we get things figured out. You'll also need at least need conditioner, probably even shampoo. Am I right? Jace had next to nothing in his bathroom. I mean, I'm not high maintenance, but a girl needs something pretty smelling." Leave it to Cassie to figure the girl out; it's what she did for a living.

Coming to a resolution, Dani scribbled some things down. Mercury didn't care if she hung out in his shirts all day. And slept in them, letting her scent permeate every fiber. He never wanted to wash the shorts she was in as it was. But she would feel better in her own stuff, and if he wasn't thinking with his dick, it'd be harder to hide weapons in the more form fitting women's apparel.

"Cassie, Jace, I need your input," Mercury debated on bringing it up here, but he had to know what they might be up against, and he wanted to bring it to the commander as soon as possible.

"Sure," they said in unison.

Would Mercury and Dani ever be like them—happily mated? First, they had to find out more about the baby and if Dani was who she claimed.

"You said you could feel Madame G's presence when she mated you." Mercury began. Dani looked at the pair, eyes widening. So she knew the story.

"I couldn't," Jace replied. "I know our natural mating bond feels better, but overall, not much different."

"I felt tainted, slimy," Cassie added. "Like I had to get her out of me."

"How did she incorporate herself into something like a mating bond?" Dani asked quietly.

"Blood and some fucked-up ritual," Jace answered.

"Why? Do you feel something off about the pregnancy, Dani?" Cassie asked.

"Not other than an unnatural taste for bacon." Dani's brows furrowed, her gaze dropped to the tabletop. "But it's so early yet."

She glanced up to Mercury with a questioning look. He shuttered his face, unwilling to tell her what he'd felt earlier in front of Jace and Cassie.

"We'd better get going. I've gotta shadow Cassie while she's working in case Sigma tries anything again," Jace said, grabbing their food containers and to-go cups.

Even as the couple left, Dani didn't look away from Mercury. She didn't seem as fatigued and drawn as last night. Despite the nightmares, the food and rest did her good. And though it was a short night and early morning, a healthy glow lit her from within.

"What aren't you telling me?" she asked.

"What aren't you telling me?" he countered.

Setting her jaw, she looked down at her plate. "Do you think that madwoman has somehow tied herself to the baby?"

"It would be naïve not to think that." Mercury took a deep breath. He didn't feel like she was lying about this, she really didn't know what Madame G could have done. "We connected outside and, yes, I felt something, faint, but dark. Something other than you and the young one."

Blood drained from her face and she closed her eyes.

"What do we do?" she whispered.

"Tell Commander Fitzsimmons my suspicions."

Nodding slightly, her intelligent dark eyes inspected Mercury's face. He sat still under her perusal, sensing she was about to say something.

"Why do they say you're weird, Mercury?"

His brows shot up, surprised at her blunt question. He took a short moment to savor his name rolling off her tongue before he answered.

"It's how I was raised. The quintessential boy raised by wolves. Master Bellamy found me out in the wild, living with a pack of natural born wolves. I have no memory before the wolf pack took me in. Master Bellamy assumed my pack was destroyed as a young boy. I somehow survived and was taken in by a perceptive wolf pack that seemed to sense what I was."

"But, wouldn't you have been in human form until puberty?"

"Yes. After the first transition, I rarely went back to my human form. It was easier, then, living with them. I didn't know what I was, just that I was different."

"Is that how you feel now?" No pity, no derision, she seemed to want to understand him.

"Yep. Master Bellamy, at the time he was the commander, found me when he was out on a mission and realized I was not only a shifter, but born to be a Guardian." Mercury remembered being absolutely fascinated, but threatened, by this man who could also take on two forms. And utterly perplexed that the master would pick the inferior of the two to remain in much of the time.

"He and his mate took me in," Mercury continued. "Taught me to adjust to being mostly human with a beast inside, instead of the other way around. Taught me to fight in both forms and trained me to be a Guardian. Once I met Bennett and Fitzsimmons, I started learning how to interact as a human better. But it's difficult. Our job keeps us busy, usually dealing with the shit of the species and, until the last few decades, we all tried to avoid modern society. I still don't understand normal social interaction very well, even if it's shifters in human form."

Processing her astonishment of his life's story, she considered what she heard.

"So…few possessions but books?"

"I never went to school, but Master Bellamy's mate taught me to read. It helps me to have a reference with people when I can associate expressions with words that are said. I'm teaching myself the other subjects as time allows."

It looked like more questions were lining up in her sharp, sexy brain but Mercury had to cut her off.

"It's time to go talk with the commander."

***

"I said I would tell you everything, just let me type it. It'd be faster." Dani was beyond irritated. Were they really so not used to their prisoners confessing that they couldn't hand over a damn pencil and paper? She was probably being recorded anyway. Enough with the questions already.

Commander Fitzsimmons pinned her with that unreadable look she was beginning to associate with him. He was such a serious dude, his smile muscles had probably atrophied.

"You're going to write everything down? Just like that?" Disbelief obvious in his tone. Another thing she began to associate with him. He probably had a dry sense of humor, if he had one at all.

"You can't protect me and this kid unless you know what you're up against. Unless you've been in the compound before, it'd be faster if I drew diagrams and explained the rooms. Then I can describe the Agents and the training, what I know of it."

Another long considering look. "Fine. We'll cross reference it with what we already have on file. Mercury, stay with her."

Dani wanted to breathe a sigh of relief with the commander gone. That was an intense man. The cloud of tension dissipated with his absence. Even more so after Mercury brought his concerns to him about the extra presence he felt when they connected outside.

The thought filled Dani with terror. Was a part of Madame G inside of her? Was it like a tracking device? Of course Sigma knew where she was, but they'd get lost wandering the woods with all the defenses around the lodge and land around the cabins. But the hope that Dani and her baby could mosey off, undetected, when they were both recovered and healthy, died a slow death.

Was she really Mercury's mate or was that orchestrated by the evil bitch, too? That bothered Dani, for unknown reasons. She wasn't ready to tie her life to him by any means, but it was undeniable that she felt something for him. Not just gratitude for rescuing her, or the care he'd taken of her, or the way his body felt on hers, his fingers inside of her.

Desire began to pool in her belly, Mercury inhaled sharply.

"We'd better get you drawing," his deep voice rougher than normal.

The few bad shifters Sigma and its Agents took out did not make up for the pain and suffering the secret corporation and its most notorious chapter leader, Madame G, inflicted on both shifters and humans. And probably vampires, although Dani avoided them as much as possible. They made her feel like she was on the menu.

***

Two weeks passed in a relatively boring manner and Dani loved it. After her violent last few years, wondering if she'd survive and escape Sigma's clutches, her future terribly uncertain, she reveled in the quiet days of research.

The Guardians were researching all the information and details she gave them on Sigma's compound, the Agents, and their training program. Commander Fitzsimmons took their concerns of Madame G's baby tampering seriously and was trying to get details of how, how badly, and how the hell to fix it.

Dani was currently combing through the latest pregnancy literature. Unfortunately, there was no manual for *What to Expect When You're Expecting a Different Species* or *What to Expect When Your Baby Might Be Possessed.*

She was given limited access to the internet and her web trail was carefully monitored by the asshole Mason and his derogatory human comments. She gave the most ashamedly girly squeal when Mercury showed her his e-reader and the books he'd downloaded for it.

Mercury.

Even now watching him face-off in the training gym with Kaitlyn, whom she couldn't help but soften toward, he made her heart flutter. Sweat dotted his brow and he was giving almost inaudible instructions to the female shifter during their sparring. The woman was fast and strong, but Mercury's skills were completely "amazeballs," using his own word. Dani suspected he loved messing with Bennett, picking up the trending vernacular and incorporating it into his daily language. The others probably thought it was part of the male's troubles with socializing, but Dani suspected differently. He was painfully blunt at times, yes, but also subtly mischievous and more highly functioning than anyone gave him credit for, including himself.

Right now he had the female in a headlock that would have decapitated Dani. Kaitlyn was struggling, trying to maneuver her feet around his to yank them out from under him. No jealousy spiked at the contact and Dani was relieved. The rage-inducing jealously she experienced regarding Mercury's past seemed to die away the more she got to know him.

It was obvious he took Kaitlyn's training seriously, as did all the other Guardians, and like the rest, he didn't treat her any differently. They all rotated training with each other, sometimes fighting two or three against one. They kept her from Master Bellamy's training, not trusting her with their secrets, but it was all good. Dani picked up quite a few of her own survival tips to file away for any future hand-to-hand combat.

Kaitlyn's face was turning a nasty shade of blue, her efforts dwindling. Dani stopped beating at the punching bag she was half-assing to watch the scene unfold, her heart in her throat. Finally, with one final exertion, Kaitlyn managed to drop

Mercury before she passed out. It bothered Dani every time she witnessed their comebacks. Was it because they trained that hard that they nearly killed each other? Or was it because if it was her, she'd be dead and stay dead? Yes and yes. Unless she mated Mercury, then it would take decapitation or silver to end her life.

The male still didn't trust her. Hadn't touched her since that morning after she arrived. She was in the most sexually frustrated state she ever thought possible, having to see him every day, all day, with little to no physical contact. Each night she went to bed alone, while he slept on the porch with his back to the door. And each morning he was on the front steps, his arms resting on his knees waiting for her to wake up.

After she'd confessed everything she was willing to, she was informed Mercury would be her keeper until further notice. It only took one day of shadowing him until she started making demands: reading and exercise, at the minimum. She would have volunteered to take a shift cooking, but knew better than to ask, as they'd fear her poisoning the food. Laundry duty was even forbidden to her and at this point, Mercury's cabin was as clean as it could possibly be.

He watched her. She bet he thought she didn't notice. Cassie had brought back workout clothes galore, from form fitting to loose and comfy. Leaving loose and comfy for the later trimesters, Dani ran in a running bra and capri leggings. The daily laps around the lodge were getting pretty tedious, but she wasn't allowed anywhere else. Mercury trailed her and she felt the burn like Superman's laser vision going right into her ass. Maybe she shook it just a little extra on the straight stretches.

Her most satisfying moment to date as a young, single, attractive female was one day in front of the cabin when she busted out the yoga mat she borrowed from the training gym. Sliding effortlessly through remembered vinyasa sequences, enjoying the stretch of muscles she hadn't felt in years, she became acutely aware of Mercury's sudden stillness. He'd decided to clean gear while babysitting her sudden urge for yoga, but she hit the first downward dog and he was done. With no movement, his eyes swept her body as she flowed from position to position.

Now she did yoga every damn day.

"Daniella?" A voice interrupted her musings, causing her to jump. Then a shiver ran through her, like it always did when she heard her full name spoken by that deep voice.

Kaitlyn had already left the gym and Mercury had removed his sweat-soaked shirt. Dani was almost afraid to look, afraid she wouldn't quit ogling his chest, afraid she'd start tracing his muscles with her fingertips and get bolder from there.

"Ready?" Mercury interrupted her musings again.

"Yep." Her thoughts returned to the present moment to take off the boxing gloves they let her use and follow him through the lodge back to the cabin.

It was early evening but the gathering clouds made it seem later.

"It's going to storm?" she asked him.

Mercury nodded and answered without a pause. "It'll last all night."

Dani found she wasn't surprised by the information. She suspected the little peanut in her body gave her intuition a boost. With normal human senses, she could tell a storm was building, but had no way to tell the duration or severity without special training. Shifters just knew what the weather was going to do, they were so attuned to nature.

Deciding to make notes of the unusual feelings and occurrences that had happened in the last month of pregnancy, Dani would add "better weather radar" to the list, along with her two wishes that came true, and homicidal rage and jealousy regarding the tall, heavily muscled male walking in front of her.

Holding the door to the cabin open for her, he said, "I'm just going to clean up before I turn in."

That was her cue to hang out in the kitchen while Mercury used the bathroom and dressed. This was their standard routine—awkwardly waiting while the other cleaned up. She knew they both felt the drive to join the other in the shower, and not bothering to towel off before making their way to the bed together.

Maybe she'd have to note "increased sexual frustration" on her list. Her breasts were tender, probably a first trimester issue, but she longed for Mercury's calloused hands to massage them. Not struggling much with nausea or fatigue since Mercury made sure she got as much rest as she needed, the only major pregnancy symptom Dani noted was the monster craving for bacon. The absence of common expectant mom woes left her body open to desire. A lot of desire. For the naked male in the shower.

Getting a yogurt and thinking she'd kill for a greasy burger, Dani sat and waited. The sky opened up, dumping large, fat droplets of rain on the cabin. Was he still going to sleep out on the porch in this weather? The rain was steadily increasing and peals of thunder in the distance could be heard. This was the first overnight storm since she arrived and she wondered if the sleeping arrangements would change. She hoped they would.

Mercury came around the corner wearing nothing but athletic shorts. No lights were on yet and shadows cast through the room from the flashes of lightning outside gave him a dark menacing air as silver flashed through his features.

"Goodnight, Daniella." He reached for the door.

"Wait!" Dani abandoned her yogurt and stood. "You aren't going to sleep out in that, are you?"

"It's not so bad. I'll sleep a little closer to the building, but there's a big overhang. Even if it rains on me," he shrugged, "it's not a big deal. I've slept in worse."

She closed the distance to stand in front of him. "But you don't have to. Why don't you stay in here?"

Lightning highlighted his features again. Silver swirled in his eyes, his jaw was clenched as he considered her, his hand tight on the door handle.

"That wouldn't be a good idea."

She moved even closer, looking up at him. He was so still, she wondered if he was even breathing.

"Why not?"

"Because I need the door between us to remind me to stay away from you." His voice sounded strangled. She saw the conflict raging within. His body, judging from the heat radiating from him, wanted to stay. His brain was telling him to go out as fast as he could and let the rain cool him off.

Putting her hands on his chest, he sucked in a breath, she stood on her tiptoes, her lips inches from his. She shouldn't do this, shouldn't tempt this beast that was her mate. But she wanted him, her body burned for him.

"Stay with me tonight, Mercury."

The growl rumbled through her fingertips and he captured her mouth. Dani leaned into the kiss and wrapped her arms around his thick neck, pressing her body against the length of him, twining her tongue around his. At last. For weeks, she felt empty, bereft, though he was always with her. Her body *needed* him.

Mercury skated his hands down her body, lifted her against him, and walked to the bed. Not needing to open his eyes or break contact with her mouth, he sat on the edge of the bed with Dani straddling him. His hard arousal pressed into her, its heat teasing her body where she wanted him most.

Dani wasn't like this, chalk it up to pregnancy hormones. For years, she hadn't dated—not even kissed during her quest for vengeance. Before that, she was gladly what one would call a tease, only granting a few the status of boyfriend, but always they were the pursuer and she'd made them work for it. Life had been lived on her terms, the privileged daughter of a doting father and a super intelligent mother.

But this? This was different. And there were too many clothes in the way. Her shirt had to go. Wishing she could rip it off so she didn't have to break contact with her male, she quickly pulled it over her head. Mercury stilled, his eyes roaming her torso, the silver gleam didn't need to be highlighted by flashes of lightning, reflecting instead like a predator locked onto his prey.

"Beautiful."

She barely heard the word float the short distance to her. She gave him a small smile, almost shy now under his wondrous perusal.

"But this has to go." Running his fingers under the straps of her bra, they skimmed the tops of her breasts. Willing herself to be patient, soon she would have his hands on her, cupping and massaging her tender swells, she let him explore.

His fingers burned a trail over her sensitized skin around to her back and attempted to undo the clasp. A crease formed on his brow as he concentrated on his task. A low, frustrated growl rumbled through him as his fingers fumbled with the hooks. Dani let out a burst of laughter.

"Here, let me." Reaching back, she had her bra unhooked and off in less than two seconds. Letting it fall to the ground, she watched his reaction.

He let out a whoosh of air, the silver fire swirling through his dark eyes, focused on her breasts. His hands around her ribcage slid up to cup her tender breasts. Moaning she arched into him, the heat of his hands easing the tenderness. His thumb and forefinger caressed her taut nipples and she let out a little moan. At last.

Her moan deepened when he dipped his head down, closing his mouth over one tip. As if he sensed exactly what her body wanted him to do, he gently kneaded each breast while his tongue explored every curve.

The thunder outside barely masked her pounding heart. She'd been wanting this shifter's touch since she first laid eyes on him. Their first morning together wasn't nearly enough. She wanted to taste him.

Pushing against his shoulders, he brought his head up to look questioningly at her, afraid he'd done something wrong.

Putting both hands on the side of his face, she said, "My turn."

Giving him a slow sensuous kiss, she trailed kisses down his neck, reveling in the shivers rippling through him. Sliding off his lap, down to her knees before him, she kept burning a path over his rippled chest and stomach with her mouth. When she reached under the waistband of his shorts, he stopped her hands with his own and froze.

"What are you doing?" He sounded almost horrified.

"I want to taste you."

"No. You're not like them. You're not a jelly girl." He was shaking his head emphatically.

"A what?"

"That's what Cassie called the girls we were with at the club. Because they walked like their legs were made of jelly after they were done with us."

Seriously? Dani gave a snort of derision, that was actually kinda funny.

"This isn't the club. I'm not a random girl. I want you in my mouth, Mercury." With that, she slid his waistband down over his impressive size and down his long length. When it sprang free, her eyes widened a little, a bit apprehensive about the task she intended to take on. He was a large man, thick and long.

He remained frozen. Dani was determined. She had a drive to not only please him, but wipe out any memory remaining of anyone else who might have done this for him. Call it pride, jealousy, whatever—she was going to blow his mind, regardless that she had little practice at this specific task. Going down on a guy had been one of those things that she wanted to experience and once done, never had the urge to do again. Her m.o. had been to string her boyfriends along while they waited on her every whim until she got bored and cut them loose. Dani would admit shallow would have been a good word to describe her before her parents were killed.

Keeping eye contact, she reached for him. His hot length soothed the raging need coursing through her. He was like velvet-covered steel, the smooth skin felt good under her fingers. Stroking him up and down, she broke eye contact and leaned forward, first licking the tip before wrapping her lips around the broad head. Her eyes dropped closed, loving the intimacy this act brought to their tentative, budding relationship.

The breath Mercury had been holding whooshed out. Air got sucked back in just as quickly when she began a languid rhythm, up and down, long slow lick, up and down, repeat. He tensed and relaxed, as if he didn't know what to do with her. He was afraid she'd keep going, but terrified she'd quit. Dani kept up her suckling rhythm, stroking the base of his shaft with one hand, and cupping and massaging his sac with the other.

Mercury tunneled his hands carefully through her hair, allowing himself small thrusts into her, but careful not to tug or pull at her. His breathing was rougher and quicker, and somehow she knew he hadn't taken his eyes off her for one second.

Low groans and grunts filled any silence between thunderclaps and his hands tightened on her hair.

"Sweet Mother Earth, Daniella. I'm going to come," he rasped.

She locked on tighter, creating more suction with each movement. The hands abruptly left her hair and gripped the side of the bed. Mercury's roar echoed through the cabin; He pulsed within her mouth, under her hands, and hot jets hit the back of her throat before she swallowed him down.

Left shaking and panting, Mercury was almost slumped over her when she let him go and sat back on her knees. Recovering quickly, he slid down to his knees in front of her, wrapped her up in his strong embrace and kissed the ever-loving hell out of her. Dani didn't have any time to react before he picked her up and laid her back.

The cool wood floor was a nice contrast to his burning body above her. As soon as he settled her on the floor, he moved with kisses down her body stopping at each breast to lick and nuzzle only long enough for him to work her yoga pants down her legs and off her body.

Settling in between her knees, he kissed and tasted his way down until his face was level with her core. Then… nothing.

Frowning slightly, Dani propped herself up on her elbows and looked down at him. His covetous look of reverence made her feel like the most special present that had ever been offered to the male. It was like he had never seen a woman like this, and she remembered he probably hadn't, and what he saw he was in absolute awe of.

His dark, gleaming eyes flicked up to her. "This. Is. Mine."

He pulled her against his mouth and gave her a long stroke with his tongue. Dani's arms almost gave out, she dropped her head back and moaned. His inexperienced, yet extremely talented tongue found her pleasure center quickly and locked on.

Dani's arms finally gave way and she laid out flat on the floor while Mercury worked her center. Writhing against him, she let out a cry when he inserted one thick finger into her. The slide of his digit and the strokes from his tongue were a superb combination building the need inside of her until she thought she would explode. Each cry she let out in hopes it would dull the impending heart-stopping release.

Then he quirked his finger within and she was done. Her cry turned into a wail, she shook and shuddered against Mercury but he didn't let up. Pleasure overtook her mind, her body already surrendered to the exotic shifter; waves of ecstasy rolled over her, rendering her nearly catatonic.

"Enough," she finally gasped, pushing at his mercury-tinted hair.

Wiping his mouth with the back of his hand, he reared over her. Shadows danced off his tanned skin, highlighting the ridges of his heavily muscled torso. He was still hard, even after what Dani had done for him. Not contained by his athletic shorts, he appeared even harder and bigger than before.

This was it. She would finally be joined with the father of her baby. Finally feel like there was meaning, a connection to support the conception, to bring her healing for how it had happened.

She reached her arms out to beckon him into her embrace, when a panicked look crossed his face.

"I can't do this to you."

"Do what?" she asked, thoroughly confused.

"You're so small. I'll hurt you or the baby with my inexperience." He jumped to his feet, covered himself with his shorts and slammed out the door into the pouring rain before she could utter a word of objection.

Chapter Seven

Mercury ran straight up the hill behind his cabin, noting with dismay that the rain was washing her scent off him. His mate. His mate he couldn't trust, but wanted with every fiber of his being. The last couple of weeks had been torture. His only respite were the nights sleeping under the stars, with the door between them to mute her intoxicating orange blossom scent.

His bare feet pounded the worn path that led from his cabin to the shifter he sought out. He knew the way by heart.

Chest heaving, need and regret pounding through him, rain running in rivulets down his chest, he pounded on the door.

It swung open and the attractive blonde female that answered stepped aside for Mercury, who stopped on the welcome mat and went no further.

She shut the door behind him, concern on her face. "Let me get you a towel, wildling." Striding away with her unhurried gentle sway, her bare feet under her simple shift barely made a sound.

Relieved, he could sense they were alone. This was not something he wanted another pair of sensitive ears to overhear.

Handing him the towel, she stood back with her arms crossed, giving him time to dry off. Her eyes took in his disheveled form from head to toe. He could imagine what her intuitive gaze picked up on: distrust, fear, sexual frustration, and worst of all—insecurity.

"Come. Let's have some tea and talk."

Irina Bellamy was like a surrogate mother to him. When Master Bellamy rescued Mercury all those generations ago, he brought the wild-eyed Mercury to his home where his formidable, patient wife taught Mercury the beginnings of how to live like a human who can shift into a wolf, not like he'd been living—a wolf that can turn human.

They formed a close bond during those first few years and although he hardly ever saw her anymore, despite their relatively close living arrangement, she was the only one he wanted to go to with personal troubles. His most trusted advisor on all things female.

Smelling dandelion tea, Mercury was taken back to his early days with the older female. When he first came to the Guardian pack, she was a maternal figure for many of the shifters in the pack. Guardians were the only family to each other, entering training after puberty, and with their way of life, tragedy had often struck. It created a strong bond of brotherhood and mates were often a part of the connection.

Master Bellamy had brought Mercury back to Guardian camp and Irina immediately opened her heart to embrace the wild shifter and help him adapt to the human world. From there, he formed his own connections with the other shifters, the strongest with his partner of almost a century, Bennett. Things were good, he was learning, they weathered some hard times, and then tragedy struck the Bellamys eventually causing Master Bellamy to hand over commander reins to Fitzsimmons, and Irina to withdraw slowly over time.

The move to West Creek seemed to be the final straw. Becoming a recluse in her own cabin, she no longer cooked for them or encouraged drop-in visits. The Guardians moved on, dealing with the world in their own way. Mercury doubted even Irina and Master Bellamy's paths crossed much, and that was highly unusual for a previously closely mated couple. A couple that had weathered centuries together and mentored young shifters through tragic events, they were devastated by a tragedy that not even their love for each other could repair.

"Are you well, wilding?" Irina asked, maternal concern highlighting her words.

Mercury shook his head. "It's her."

"Ah," she nodded slowly, staring blankly at her hands wrapped around her mug. "How do you feel about her?"

Lifting one muscled shoulder in a half shrug, Mercury didn't know where to begin. "Crazy."

A small smile lifted the corner of Irina's mouth. "That's a start."

"I want her. So bad. I almost took her tonight. I've wanted to claim her since I laid eyes on her, since before I scented my young within her. But I was afraid I would hurt her and the baby."

Irina pursed her lips and gave Mercury a considering look, then chuckled softly, "Unless you're picking her up and throwing her across the room, you're not going to hurt her. You've seen enough sexual encounters to know that human women don't break. But that's not really the problem, is it?"

"No."

A stretch of silence followed, the rain continued to pour outside. Irina waited.

"You don't trust her."

Mercury shook his head, staring dismally at the cabin floor.

"For many that wouldn't matter," Irina prodded gently.

"No. It wouldn't."

They sat again in silence.

"She's hiding something. From me and from the others. I can barely keep myself away from her. Her scent drives me crazy. If I claim her, it won't matter what's she's hiding. I'd destroy anyone who tried to hurt her. No matter who it is. She'd own me."

Irina wouldn't need him to go into specifics, he was confident she picked up on the unspoken truth. He'd turn against his own pack even as Dani was knifing him in the back.

"Have more faith in yourself, and your brothers. They will protect you, even if it's from yourself."

Mercury mulled her words over. Irina was right. If only it was the only fear that drove him from his mate's warm and willing body.

"What else is bothering you, Mercury?" It was a tense question, as if she knew the direction this conversation was going to was a dark place she didn't want to ever visit again.

Irina could read him all those years ago when he struggled to learn words, and even worse, pair them with human emotion. She was astute enough to read into a sudden, frantic visit about his pregnant mate.

"What if we do mate and all that, but something happens to the baby?"

Irina's face turned to stone, color leeching slowly from her features. Mercury would agree when those close to him claimed he was dense when it came to feelings, but even he knew this topic was devastating. But there was no one else he could turn to.

"Well," Irina said flatly, "if you mate and she's not a traitor and the babe is yours and…" she paused for a deep, cleansing breath, "and the child is ripped away," her voice cracked, "then by whatever is holy in your life, don't abandon her to deal with the emptiness alone."

"I would never do that," Mercury said, horrified at the thought of leaving Dani to suffer the loss of a child on her own.

"A male's need for vengeance can override good sense. Remember that." Irina abruptly stood up, walked to the door and opened it, looking expectantly at Mercury, an obvious sign it was time for him to go.

He stepped out, the porch overhang protecting him from the downpour. The hair on his arms stood up and his sensitive ears honed in on sounds he could make out between the thunderclaps.

Dani! Leaving his shorts in a pile on the Bellamy's porch, he let his beast break free. The giant black wolf tore into the night.

***

Completely taken aback, Dani had scrambled for her clothes as soon as the door swung shut. She knew he didn't stop at the porch to turn in for the night. He was gone.

Realistically, she knew she shouldn't go after him. It was storming and she didn't have the enhanced senses or speed of the shifter she was searching for. But fuck it, she couldn't just sit in the cabin waiting for him to return at his leisure. And when he did, it would be most likely to not explain what made him run, after giving her the most earth-shattering orgasm a human body could tolerate.

Getting her clothes right side out and back on, she paused only to grab one of his black waterproof jackets from the tiny coat closet by the front door and throw on her running shoes. She headed out into the rain, the hood from the too big coat giving her ample protection, for her head at least. Her shoes and lower legs would quickly be soaked.

Carefully running to the back door of the lodge, she peeked in without opening the door. It would draw too much attention and Mason, the asshole, always seemed to be lurking around the corner waiting to get a shot at insulting her when Mercury wasn't close enough to hear. She never said anything, just ignored the disturbed shifter. But damned if she'd be to blame for causing tension between two Guardians. It would just cast doubt on her intentions.

Turning to face the dark surrounding woods in the pouring rain, she stopped to think. She always saw Bennett head off to the right and that was the most logical place Mercury would go. They had that bromance thing going on so who else would he talk about girl troubles with?

Dani had never been to Bennett's cabin. It was tucked so far back into their surroundings, she could barely make it out on a clear day. The cabins were meant to be individual dwellings for Guardians and their families, therefore, they weren't built on top of each other. Making her way in the dark, she headed back in the direction of Mercury's cabin, and then veered off in the dark in her best guess of the direction of Bennett's residence.

Her feet squished through the grass and dirt between the trees. She could only see as far as the next flash of lightning, which helped ensure she didn't smack face first into trees or low hanging branches.

Several minutes passed and Dani was breathing hard, slipping and sliding along the upward slant of the landscape. She had to be almost there. Frustrated, she stopped, waiting for several lightning flashes to light the area around her. It all looked the same. Dark tree after dark tree. Fuck! Was she lost?

Officially soaked from the knees down, water streaming off the edge of her hood, a chill worked its way into her that had little to do with being out in the rain and more to do with being lost while Sigma was out looking for her. She should've asked Cassie to pick up a flashlight because she'd rather have that than fresh underwear right now.

"Mercury!" She'd rather have all the Guardians clued in to their couple drama than have any Agents find her out here, alone and unarmed.

"Mercury!" Should she turn around and head back? How did she know she went in a straight line in the first place? Was she even close to a cabin?

A low chuckle rumbled through the rain behind her. Dani spun around with a gasp.

"Well, well, well. Little Red Riding Hood lost in the woods. Couldn't find Grandma's house?" A wicked sneer pulled at Mercury's mouth.

Not knowing what to say, Dani kept quiet. He could probably hear how hard her heart was beating. She thought Sigma finding her was bad. At least they would keep her alive for the baby. With Mason, she wasn't so sure.

"You passed right through our security barriers, human. Mercury hasn't claimed you yet, or marked you, and I set them up so you could leave whenever you wanted. I just need to make sure you don't come back."

"Why do you hate me so much?"

Mason gave a nonchalant lift of his shoulders. "It's not you personally. It's your humanity. We don't want it in our bloodlines. Purity is our key to strength. First Jace mates with a human, and brings her to live with us, no less. But he's not a born Guardian, so I overlooked it. She'll meet with a tragic accident soon enough."

Dani's mind raced. Her body screamed it should run, attack, something. Her mind told her that Mason was revealing way too much and she needed to pay attention. It also told her that he didn't intend for her to survive this encounter if he wasn't monitoring his words.

"But then you show up and a *Guardian* chooses you, a human, for his mate," Mason continued. "And even worse, you're going to reproduce and dull his lines. The purity of his power is staggering, though more than a little unfocused. We can't have human taint on it."

Pulling a gun out of his waistband, he pointed it at her.

She licked dry lips, "So that's it. You're just going to shoot me and think they won't know. We might not be mated, but Mercury will hunt you down."

"Sorry, sweetheart. I got this off a Sigma recruit. It'll look like I came up on the scene, and saw you trying to get back to Sigma, but they took you out rather than letting us have you."

When he raised it a little higher to pull the trigger, she blurted, "I wish you dropped the gun!"

A momentary *what the fuck* look crossed his face before disbelief when the pistol ripped out of his hand and hit the ground.

Mason pinned her with a stunned look. "You shouldn't be able to do that."

Her triumphant moment was only fleeting.

He held eye contact. "Just stand there while I kill you with my bare hands," he growled, using his compulsion on her.

Her body stilled as if frozen to the ground. *No, no, no!* She had to defend herself.

Mason lunged, bringing his hands up to wrap them around her throat. With a hard mental twist, she undid his compulsion and kicked out. Her soaked foot hit him squarely in the abdomen and she ducked under his reach, dancing out of the way.

"Wha—" The breath whooshed out of him. "You shouldn't be able to do any of this," he gasped. He quickly spun grabbing her arm and pulled her to him. She kicked and hit, but he was ready for her attack and the soggy ground gave her little purchase for fighting.

Dani was turned until her back was against his front, with his elbow locked solidly around her throat. Air was squeezed out of her, none able to return. She kept kicking back and jabbing him with her elbows, but the mountain of steel holding her didn't budge.

I wish he'd drop me! His grip loosened for a split second, allowing her to draw in just a little air, but he recovered quickly fighting off her wish.

Her short life flashed through her mind when it stopped on this morning. Rain pelted her face, and while his clothing seemed to resist the soaking, hers did not. She was slick and slippery and it was still pouring. Her strength was waning, but unlike Kaitlyn's final effort, hers would be fueled by the panic of knowing she wouldn't come back from strangulation.

Twisting her feet back to hook behind his legs, extra strength poured into her movements as she jerked his feet out from under him.

He toppled back in surprise, his arm loosening around her neck enough for her to slide out and roll away. Springing up into a fighting crouch, she faced him.

Mason recovered nearly as fast as she did and was on his feet, lunging for her again, when a blast rang though rain-laden air and he went flying backward, a gaping hole in his chest.

Dani's eyes widened, hope surging through her. Had Mercury found her?

"Silver. Gets 'em every time." The familiar female voice was definitely not Mercury's.

Hope died a slow death within Dani. She searched through the dark trees and saw Agent X with her shoulder propped against a tree trunk. Her vivid green eyes flashed with their predator's gleam, her usually crazy hair laid flat by the rain, with streaming rivulets of water running down her ivory face.

"Nice shootin', Biggie." X nodded to Agent E, who was somewhere behind Dani. "Gotta say, doll, that baby's giving you some fierce shifter juice to face off against a Guardian."

Dani still couldn't see E, but knew he was getting closer.

"What did she do to my baby, X? What did Madame G do?" Dani tried to get some information before she faced another struggle. Her body ached from Mason's attack, her throat raw, and now she was facing two Agents. Not just any two, either. Two that knew her abilities and taught her what little she knew.

A look of dismay highlighted X's beautiful features. "Of course she did something, doll. She's tied to the baby somehow, like a really wicked fairy godmother."

"How do I get her out of me?"

"And why would we tell you that?" E's deep timbre came from right behind her.

She spun around. He held no weapon anymore and wasn't crouched to attack her. His hands were tucked into his waistband like they'd all just met to chat in the middle of the dark woods during a major storm.

"Because not even you two would want to see an innocent baby used this way. Of all people, you know what she's capable of."

"Madame G's depravity surprises me sometimes, I have to admit. But no one knows what she's really capable of," X informed her, then cocked her head at Dani. "Or why."

The wind suddenly picked up, tearing through the trees, strong enough to lift soggy leaves and broken branches. Dani's legs and face stung as they pelted her.

"Uh oh," X's eyes glinted in the dark. "Who let the dogs out?"

Wind and rain whipped around Dani's face. Mercury was on his way. She could feel him in the power flowing around her before she heard the howls buffeting through the wind.

Agent E moved to grab her from behind and she ducked and spun out of his reach, slipping easily away since he couldn't get a good purchase on her slippery, wet coat. Although they wouldn't kill her and would try not to hurt the baby, she was at a definite disadvantage with the slick ground, her human eyes having trouble making out the Agents.

It was like a sixth sense kicked in, along with her previous training. She couldn't see X or E very well, but they were there and she guessed their moves before they were made. Over and over, they lunged in for her and Dani spun, kicked, jabbed, and danced out of their reach. Much of it was her previous training with these very Agents, the rest though...

She heard Mercury's howl in the wind. He was only seconds away.

The two dangerous Agents made one final attempt to grab her and haul her away. They'd have to run and run fast. It wasn't just Mercury coming to her rescue. More howls filtered through the wind.

X's strong hands wrapped like steel around Dani's wrists, trying to twist her around while E was targeting her feet. Both Agents had bindings of some sort and Dani had to keep out of them.

When the hard metal closed around one wrist, she reacted, "I wish it'd fall off."

The cuffs slid off. Dani sprang out from between a startled X and a crouching E, landing poorly and losing her footing. She twisted her body as she fell, using the motion of a front roll to carry her even farther away from the Agents.

The howls were on top of them now. She felt, more than saw, the Agents disappearing into the night. Their goal of her capture would not be fulfilled tonight.

"You were a good Agent, doll," X called back, the wind carrying her words clearly. "I'll miss our time hunting shifters."

Oh. Shit.

Dani knew the time would come when the major detail she'd been omitting would be revealed. She'd just hoped that when it did, Mercury and the other Guardians would trust her enough to listen to the rest of the story. She seriously doubted they'd reached that point yet.

He stopped just feet away from where she crouched in the rain. Her eyes met the swirling, shining eyes of the familiar mammoth black wolf.

Two more large wolves were highlighted by the lightning behind Mercury. With stunning synchronicity, they flowed from their wolf state into stunning human males. They were several inches taller than Mercury with longer brown hair plastered to their identical chiseled faces and their eyes were probably brown when they weren't highlighted by the hunter's shine. Like the rest of the Guardians, they were heavily muscled and devastatingly handsome. And naked.

"The Agents are gone. Those bastards run fast," informed one of the twins in a deep baritone. His gaze locked onto her. "Or should I say, most of the Agents are gone."

"I'm not an Agent," Dani rushed to explain.

"Did you or did you not hunt shifters?" Bennett's voice from behind her spooked her, but she didn't spin around. He was probably naked, too, having transitioned already. Only Mercury remained in his wolf state, his unblinking gaze locked onto her.

"Only the ones that killed my family. And they were feral."

"How many of us have you killed?" the same twin who spoke before asked.

"There were three who were responsible for my parent's death," Dani hedged, still unwilling to get to the complete truth.

"And how many of us did you *kill*?" Bennett asked, from between clenched teeth.

Dani swallowed and hoped it wouldn't be all black and white with them.

"There were two others, also feral. The three that took out my family were part of the deal I made when I joined Sigma."

A sharp inhale from Bennett spoke volumes.

"I would join to become an Agent if they allowed me to take out those males. By the time I was done hunting the feral males, I had seen enough. Realized I made a mistake, then…" She looked at Mercury, pleading with him to believe her.

"Then they decided to make you an incubator for one of our abominations?" Bennett said with a caustic tone.

That made Dani angry, but before she could react, Mercury swung around and loped off into the night. The three other Guardians silently watched him, then locked their incensed gazes back in on her.

Chapter Eight

"Three drinks and that's final, X," Demetrius bargained.

"Two sips," X countered.

A slow, sensuous smile curled Demetrius' full lips and he opened the door to let her in.

X sauntered in, dropping the trench coat from her shoulders, wearing only black heels.

"I want the information before we're done."

Demetrius' eyes glittered as he scanned X's naked body. His tongue stroked one fang. "Deal. But I need to warm you up. It's been a while hasn't it? Since the last time you needed some intel?"

X's fiery green eyes narrowed, she put her hands on her hips. "The warm up counts as one sip."

A low chuckle reverberated through the big male's body.

"Fine," he agreed, closing in.

She looked up at him through her lashes as he neared. Demetrius probably started as Madame G's vampire equal, heading up this chapter of Sigma. But she far surpassed his power and no one knew how. X suspected Demetrius had insight. She also suspected his powers weren't as far surpassed as everyone thought and he was always helpful, for a price.

Taking in his shoulder length amber hair that reflected the light filtering in from the compound's exterior, his pale green eyes swept over her breasts and naked lower half, heat flaring when he noticed she still wore her heels.

There were worse missions. Fucking Demetrius for information was something she did occasionally. Getting to drink shifter blood, freely without a fight, was a rare treat for vampires with the added benefit that her strong shifter body could take the pounding of a male feeding vampire. Otherwise, they tried to separate the two. Too many casualties. She chose Demetrius, because although his motives seemed aligned with Sigma, they were still his own. In that respect, she felt a kinship. He was cruel, but not unnecessarily so. Madame G often tried to tempt him with female shifters, but he refused to force or seduce the captives. With X, he played the game of give and take.

It was a fine line X walked. To do this, she had to give up on any hopes for her own future. Walking around with the stench of a vampire on her would burn a bridge that made her heart ache. But that stench would keep her in Madame G's good graces and ward off suspicion that the evil matriarch's top pet was turning over a new leaf. Using her body was inevitable, but at least she reached a point of power where she could choose who, when, and how often.

Demetrius, wearing only black leather pants, his defined chest and chiseled abs on display, wrapped his hands around her back and slid them down to her backside, his mouth close to her neck.

"Oh, my first sip won't be from here."

Reaching down, he lifted her up from behind and set her up on his table. A single vampire didn't need a six foot dining room table for family gatherings. It was obvious he enjoyed many different courses on it.

X stretched back, allowing him to spread her legs. He knew she liked to get down to business. Don't play with breasts, don't suckle anything longer than needed, take your drink and pass the information.

He dipped his head down to her center where she was spread for him. His soft hair tickling her inner thighs. As he used his strong fingers to spread her, he looked up at her. She raised an eyebrow. He chuckled again and got to business.

Demetrius' talented tongue quickly warmed her up, but she knew he needed to prep her for his second feeding. It had indeed been awhile and this was not the male she wanted inside of her. What she wanted was irrelevant. She had one mission and one mission only. And this exchange between her and Sigma authority aided in that mission.

X leaned on her arms and rocked against Demetrius' mouth, moaning when he inserted one finger into her, quickly followed by another. The fire was stoked and rising rapidly. She held her legs apart, watching him work on her, his hair brushing her inner thighs, his arm the thrusting force behind his fingers and his tongue flicking rapidly.

X let her head fall back as she rocked with him, the moans overtaking her. When the first ripples of orgasm moved through her, Demetrious replaced his tongue with his thumb, bared his fangs and struck her inner thigh.

The intensity of the bite slammed into her and she cried out with the force.

Demetrius withdrew his fangs with her final shudders and straightened, undoing his pants. His impressive size sprang free, he kicked his pants aside and climbed up onto his knees on the table in between her legs.

He was looking greedily at her wet center when she put a heeled foot on his chest, stopping him. His eyes blazed as he looked up to her face.

"Information first, before round two. You know I'm good for it."

He inhaled sharply, wrapping a fist tightly around her ankle. A fully aroused vampire male in the middle of a feed, not yet released, could be a ferocious predator, but she didn't care. A deal was a deal.

"She tied herself to the fetus, her intention to always know where it was and when it was born, become a part of it. Like her failed attempt at mating a couple months ago, she seeks to combine herself with the child." He had finally indulged a portion of the information she sought.

Duh, of course Madame G incorporated herself into the conception somehow. That's what Madame G did.

"How?"

Demetrius shrugged a heavily muscled shoulder. "The easiest way is by blood ritual. All she'd need is a drop, it wouldn't destroy the genetic material, and would grow when conception was successful."

"So if they wanted to separate her from the bundle of joy?"

He leaned over her, his head directly above hers, placing a hand by her ear while another held himself steady for entrance. Her foot still rested on his chest, ready to stop any forward motion until she felt her question was adequately answered.

"I really don't know how they could do it. Vampires and shifters may have started walking the earth at the same time, but they took drastically different paths. One chose the dark, one chose the light. How they can remove her essence would differ with how we could remove it. I don't imagine the Guardians would place a call into any dark powers asking for advice."

His fangs were bared, his hand stroking himself, she didn't have much time.

He surprised her when he continued. "Shifters already have a way to bind to each other. I'm sure any unbinding ceremony would do the trick."

X's heart sank. The only way to unbind shifters is death and that was an unacceptable answer in this scenario.

"Why does Madame G want a baby?" she risked one final question.

He barked laughter. "Now, love. Isn't that the million dollar question?"

Moving her foot aside, he surged into her. She drew a sharp breath at the sudden fullness. Demetrius began his rhythm, his powerful buttocks clenching and undulating to move inside of her. X brought her knees higher, resting the points of her black heels into his butt cheeks, knowing he liked the jabs of pain.

Demetrius groaned, leaning his head down to lick at her neck.

"Just take your drink," she got out between pants. His thrusts increased in strength and she reached out to hang on to the edges of the heavy table. It was only temporary, once he bit, her body staying on this table would be at his discretion.

"Not ready yet." She could feel him smiling against her neck, smug bastard, his fangs scraping her super sensitive skin. He kept up his pounding rhythm, and right before he struck, he moved his hand between them to rub her clitoris, sending her over the edge.

Fangs sunk deeply into her vein. Waves of pleasure rolled over, continuously. X shut her mind off after cursing her genetic makeup, dropped her legs to the table, and let go. She was held in place by Demetrius at her neck while his frantic pumping kept her orgasm going. As long as he fed, she'd continue coming.

Skin slapping skin and Demetrius' grunts were all that could be heard until he released her, threw his head back, and roared. Veins popped out of his neck and shoulders as he strained against her, she could feel him convulsing deeply, emptying himself inside her tight channel. Unfortunately, that was another necessity of this transaction. She needed people to know who she was with, needed them to smell Demetrius on her, or they'd think she'd gotten chaste, and chaste equaled rebellion in Madame G's world. To dominate another's body was the gateway to complete mind control.

His sides still heaving, he hung his head above her. Her own fangs had slid down, they weren't always at the ready like a vampire's, thankfully, and she watched a bead of sweat trickle down the side of his neck and hover over the pulse point, beating at a rapid rate. Her tongue swirled over one fang as she eyed his vein. She wouldn't do it. Couldn't. She might have a small measure of respect for him, trust him slightly with the content of their information exchange, but she'd be stupid to trust him with who and what she really was. *That* was her only trump card. The only thing that could possibly make her suicide mission successful. Instead, she pushed lightly at his chest.

When he withdrew and climbed off the table, she sat up and did the same, donning her trench coat while he climbed into his pants.

"Good game," she said heading to the door.

"Anytime, love. I enjoy our negotiations." He walked her to the door. He couldn't help but be a gentlemen at times. "Tell me, X."

She turned to face him.

"Where do you go in your head when we're together?"

A small, sad smile lifted the corners of her mouth and she walked away.

***

Commander Rhys Fitzsimmons weaved through the club, techno dance music pounding in his chest. He was out searching for Agents or recruits to torture for information when he smelled her and whenever he smelled her, it meant trouble.

"Wanna dance?" an eager, not so young, woman asked. He regarded her with the same impassive expression he used on everyone. She gave him what was meant to be coy smile and sashayed away.

That scent. Anger coiled in his gut. He knew that specific scent of that female. He'd only smelled it a couple of times before. Rhys wove his way through the people until he reached the single bathroom in time to see a tall, dark figure disappear inside.

Bursting through the door on Demetrius' coattails, Rhys shoved the powerful vampire against the wall. A woman shrieked and cowered in the corner next to the toilet.

"Why, Commander, to what do I owe the honor?" Demetrius asked, completely unruffled by being held against the wall by his throat.

"What the fuck are you up to, Demetrius?"

"Now, now. I know how your kind tries not to draw attention to themselves. I'm just here, enjoying a good dance. I had the brunt of my aggression *squeezed* out of me earlier, leaving me free to partake of the more delicate goodies here."

Rhys glared at Demetrius, rage boiling over, squeezing the vampire's throat harder. The woman cowering behind him continued to whimper. Unable to speak and knowing he wouldn't be killed in public in front of witnesses, Demetrius allowed the commander to release some aggression.

With a snarl, Rhys released the infuriating creature and turned to go.

"It's the games we play to stay alive, Commander." Demetrius said the words as if he wanted to comfort Rhys, commiserate with him.

"One day, Demetrius, I will find out exactly what you're up to and you will pay."

"I look forward to it," Demetrius replied glibly.

Rhys marched out the door looking for the woman who approached him earlier. He found her drinking alone at the bar, scanning the crowd for more lonely males.

Her eyes lit up when she saw him heading her way. Putting her drink down and straightening her clothes, she gave him what was meant to be her most winning smile.

"I want to dance," he told her.

Almost shyly, she took his hand and followed him to an empty bathroom next to where Demetrius was successfully taking his female's mind off the confrontation.

"I don't usually do this," she admitted.

Riiight. Except he kind of believed her. She smacked of loneliness. He would know.

He closed them in the dark room and pinned her against the wall, smashing her mouth with his. His lonely woman was taken my surprise, but quickly returned his kiss with enthusiasm. When he did nothing else, just kiss her, she tentatively reached for his fly, fumbling with the buckles.

Rhys reared back. What was she doing? She'd find nothing there worth her time. He remained limp, whether through anger or the woman he was with, it didn't matter. He had to stop and think.

"Sorry, uh—I can't," he admitted.

"It's all right," she breathed, rubbing against him. "I can work on you first, if you need it."

When she dropped her knees and went back to his crotch, he batted her away.

"I need to go." He walked out, leaving the bewildered woman behind.

Leaving through the back exit, not even the dealers and the smokers loitering in the dimly lit lot attempted to mess with Rhys. The cloud of confusion and anger and menace warning them he was best left alone.

This thing with that shifter. The last time he turned to other women when he smelled X on that male, it made him feel empty and sick inside. A random fuck would do him no good and it would do the frustrating Agent no good. Whatever she was up to kept her loyal to Sigma and he was determined to find out why. Every fiber of his being screamed at him to help her, and goddammit he would, whether she needed it or not. Making himself vulnerable to getting killed while he got a blow job in some yuppie club wasn't going to help anybody.

He dedicated his life to his species. Now he dedicated it to annihilating Madame G and finding out X's secrets. Once he was appeased, then he would walk away.

Chapter Nine

Three weeks. Over three fucking weeks. Dani had been stuck in the prison cell for close to a month.

They had tried to drag her from the woods. But she clawed and fought, screaming for Mercury. Bennett had finally grabbed her like a sack of potatoes while she wailed for the massive wolf to come back. He still hadn't returned.

Three weeks. He'd been gone the entire time. She would've sensed his return, even if it was just to his cabin. Instead, she felt empty. And alone. And really bored.

Her new, and probably temporary for only nine months, sixth sense suggested she could leave at any time. Wish the prison cell door would open and voila! There was no point. She was safe in the depths of the lodge and trying to escape would only enforce the Guardians' suspicions she was guilty.

She explained everything to them, in full detail, no omissions this time. Even they sensed her honesty and sincerity. Then they locked her up.

The small room was like an economy apartment. Her dorm room in college had more amenities, but overall it wasn't a bad place to be imprisoned. It even had little windows that strategically let in the strongest rays of the day. They may have been put there to torture vampire prisoners, but they were really nice for a human prisoner.

Mason was dead. The shot to his chest was from E's special "boom stick," as she heard him call it once. It blew silver-laced ammo designed to make craters in whatever it hit. And it hit Mason square in the chest, blowing his heart into fragments and out through his back.

Mourning overtook the lodge and the Guardians. During the funeral when Dani balanced just right on the edge of her bed rails, she climbed high enough to see the rites of death carried out.

The Guardians had been devastated—sort of. Mason really was an asshole and she'd witnessed enough to know they were at a point where they didn't know if they could control the male much longer, and what they'd do if they couldn't. But he was one of them. Maybe at one time he was a decent shifter, and his death reminded them all of their own mortality.

During her interrogation, she'd told them about some of the things Mason said to her that night. Now she hoped they were investigating the former Guardian, not just her.

Kaitlyn brought Dani lunch, as she often did. And Dani was grateful. Living as a human most all of her life, unaware of her four-legged half, Kaitlyn ate like a human: carbs, fruit, and veggies.

Not just meat and more meat with a chaser of protein and a side of greasy fat like the others. Therefore, when it was her turn to cook, she fed the other Guardians more well-rounded meals than they'd seen in centuries. While the big males might grumble and complain about "shit like quinoa," Dani ate like she'd been starved, whether there was "fucking granola" fare like homemade hummus with whole wheat pita chips or rare beef roast.

After sliding the tray through the bottom slot in the door, Kaitlyn folded herself gracefully on the floor facing Dani through the bars in the door, her chin on her hands, her elbows propped on her crossed legs.

Dani sat with her eats—chicken nachos with extra sour cream. She could hear the man-bitching now. Chicken was almost a swear word at the lodge, but the shifters were coming around.

As if Kaitlyn read her thoughts, she said, "They'll never admit it now, but their human taste buds are waking up to flavors other than charred beef and pork.

Trying not to shovel in chip after loaded chip, she chewed a mouthful and raised an eyebrow at the beautiful redhead across from her.

"He's still not back," Kaitlyn announced abruptly.

Dani nodded thoughtfully, expecting as much.

The beautiful redhead narrowed her eyes slightly on Dani before saying, "Bennett's been down to Pale Moonlight looking for him."

Dani quit chewing, murderous rage roared up from her belly, pounding in her ears.

"And?" She bit out the prompt around her mouthful, glaring at the female. She heard books sliding off her nightstand and hitting the floor. One even flew across the room and hit the wall.

"There's been no sign of him," Kaitlyn smirked. Bitch.

The rage receded leaving vast relief to fill its void.

"Damn, girl. You've got it bad for the big brute."

Rage crept back in. The book on the floor could be heard sliding toward the wall, trying to catch air and take off to hit the door.

Kaitlyn looked past Dani, watching the books with amusement. "Sensitive much? You know I don't mean it as an insult."

The books went still.

"I know," Dani sighed. "I just get so defensive about him. And the baby's even worse."

"That little nugget packs a punch." Kaitlyn pointed to Dani's still flat belly. "You seriously never had mojo before being prego?"

"Nope. But I could think of a few times it would've been handy."

They went silent and Dani cleaned her plate. She didn't get snacks and her stomach would be rumbling something fierce before dinner. Her portions were big enough, but growing a shifter baby required a lot of fuel. Since there was almost nothing to do but read, Dani made sure to keep as fit as she could in her little prison doing floor exercises, yoga, and in-place cardio. Thank you elective college health course that required attending group fitness classes all semester. They kept her from death by boredom.

"So..." Dani began. "Why are you nice to me?"

"Have the others been mean?" Kaitlyn asked sharply.

"No, no." Dani said quickly. "Not friendly, but I get it. I deserve it. You've been downright considerate and now you're letting me know about Mercury when the others growl back when I ask."

"It's obvious you care about him and he cares about you. He'll come around. He might be a shifter but he's still a dude. I'm sure finding out about you when he thought he was figuring you out was like a double whammy to him. Those primitive emotions will work themselves out and he'll come back for you."

Dani had already come to the same conclusion, minus the coming back for her part. As the days ticked by, she feared that once he was back in the wild, in his comfort zone even after all this time, he was there to stay.

"But what about my history with Sigma, don't you hate me for that?"

"Did you kill anyone that didn't need killing?"

"No."

"Did you hurt anyone that didn't need hurting?"

"No." Dani could answer confidently. There had been plenty of opportunities, but with great fortune she was placed with Agent X and Agent E to train with and carry out her vendetta. They weren't into senseless violence and preferred to stay under the radar, concentrating only on the prey they were assigned to.

The first time, after her first kill when they were hunting the remaining two ferals, they came upon a shifter clan in the mountains that Sigma Agents had visited. It was revolting, the things she saw. It was like a scene from any movie that portrayed the mass murder of a tiny village by raiders. Bodies littered the land between huts— males, females, and children. Some still in shifter form, no chance against today's weaponry. Dani didn't care what the species, children were not evil and were off limits. Many of the adults, the way they died protecting their loved ones, didn't strike Dani as feral creatures out to play with and kill any prey that crossed their paths.

But she kept plugging away, hunting her targets. Then they crossed another village. There was no hiding from the awful truth that Dani had made a terrible mistake. She judged the whole species based on less than five minutes with the worst example of living flesh. As the years went by, and gossip flowed, Dani had felt the vice-like grip of Sigma's chains around her. Not just Sigma, either. She'd sworn herself to Madame G like all the other stupid recruits, and like all the others who woke up and smelled the spilled innocent blood, she knew she was good and completely fucked. No one had found a way out of the blood oath other than death, and that wasn't always a certainty.

"Well, you've been vetted by my bestie and I'm bored." Kaitlyn brought her knees up and wrapped her arms around them, looking like she wasn't going anywhere soon.

Thank God. Bored was an understatement. Dani desperately wanted the company.

"You mean when Cassie came by, got in my head, and made me ugly cry?" The tenacious woman's questions just went on and on. Much like today, Dani was bored and wanted the company. Until she found herself sobbing, spilling her guts on everything she ever felt and thought about life. But the devious woman didn't once raise an alarm within Dani or her little bun-in-the-oven; no books went flying, no objects hit the wall, nothing.

"She's good, right?" Kaitlyn grinned. "She was good at reading people before she hooked up with Jace. But now she can really dive into your brain."

Kaitlyn chatted with her for hours, just superficial chitchat about when they were both young and naive human girls with the only goal of dick-teasing boys and scoring fashion deals at the mall.

When Kaitlyn rose to go, Dani figured she'd better ask what had been on her mind for the last couple of days.

"I'm going to need OB appointments soon."

"Is something wrong?"

"Besides emotional outbursts that make objects go flying? No. Just from all the reading I've done with books we downloaded, it seems like regular doctor visits begin in the first trimester and I'm almost two months along. And with a half-species, I thought we should start figuring out how this is going to go."

"Hmmm," Kaitlyn mused. "You're totes right. What the hell are the boys going to want to do? I'll mention it." With a wave, Kaitlyn left.

Fatigue washed over Dani with the female's departure. She had done her workout already this morning, and read before lunch arrived, so nappy time it was.

***

When Dani woke up, she could tell it was much later in the day. Being summer, the sun was still out, but early evening had passed. And shit. Her food was cold. The tray had been slid in, surprisingly quiet so not to wake her, even though it was obvious one of the males was on delivery duty tonight based on the meatloaf and bacon combo.

And milk. They loved their milk—plain, chocolate, strawberry (gross!), it didn't matter.

Whaddaya know? Cold bacon and meatloaf hit the spot.

Now what?

Dani sat on her bed facing the wall, pondering her day. Maybe with the females at the lodge slowly accepting her, thanks to Cassie's subtle but thorough psychoanalysis, the males would come around. She would love to prep for her baby and wait for baby daddy's return in the cabin. She missed it terribly. She missed the male who used to sleep on the porch even more.

Daylight faded. This was the time Dani would turn in, needing more sleep than she used to, which was to be expected. Like the sore boobs and emotional roller coaster, tiredness came with the first trimester territory.

Flutters went through her belly. Dani shifted, letting her mind drift again in the fading daylight. Flutters, like butterflies, but she had nothing to be nervous about. What the hell?

An awareness settled into her, warming her insides, the heat spreading through her, arousing her.

Dani stood. She began to pace. *What. The. Hell?*

Shadows grew in her room, the sun being her only source of light was setting. She kept eyeballing the door.

Her normally tender breasts became increasingly sensitive. If her arousal wasn't evident with her nipples poking through her top, it was definitely made known in the friction created between her legs as she was pacing. If this kept up, tonight would be the night she lost her mind. There was no way she was getting herself off in this cell where they could rewind and watch her at any time on the surveillance tapes.

The heat grew and so did her awareness. The door.

Dani walked right up to it.

"Open."

The bolt *thunked* from within, and without a creak it swung open.

Cautiously, Dani walked out. There would be no creeping, she had nothing to hide. Shoulders squared she strode down the hallway, navigating her way through the lodge, commanding any locked doors to simply open and they did. When she reached the side exit, she hesitated.

Letting her mind relax, Dani used borrowed senses from her little bundle of joy to determine if any shifters were nearby or along the path in the woods where she was determined to go.

Receiving the all clear, she walked out the door.

***

His beard was scratchy. It'd been over a hundred years since Mercury had one and he didn't miss hair on his face. At least it was finally drying after his pseudo-shower in the little spring-fed waterfall a mile or so away from his cabin. He intended to go back, and like every time before in the last twenty-plus days, he didn't. He got closer tonight than ever, used the excuse he needed to bathe first, and then sat by the water but moving no further.

There was no need to.

She was coming to him. As soon as her scent drifted on the breeze to him, he hardened, his shaft coming to attention for all to see as he wore nothing, being nude when he ran off.

The first several days, he just ran. His feelings a jumbled mess that he couldn't make out until he began to sort through and analyze them like Irina taught him.

In between hunting and gathering—and evading his Guardian brothers—he realized it didn't matter what Dani had done with Sigma, it only mattered now that she wanted to leave them. He heard enough the night he left, and he knew without her having to tell him that she wasn't a mindless brute out to kill his kind because she could. He suspected that without the baby-making event, eventually she would have found a way to get away from Madame G and out of Sigma, or die trying. While he couldn't blame her for not telling him the complete truth, it burned that she didn't. Not just at the beginning, but as they were growing closer bit by bit.

What he was afraid of was that he would be endangering his pack because he couldn't give up his female. And he wouldn't give up his child. Then he realized his pack would have to deal and so would he.

Once all that was sorted out, he knew he needed to go home. And here he sat, a hundred and fiftyish year-old pussy sitting in the grass with an erection. What if she turned him away? What if she didn't? He should go back and tell her he wanted her and ask if she wanted him, too. He wasn't usually indecisive about what to say, just spewed words he was thinking.

Her scent got stronger and his hard-on got harder. In the twilight, she was coming straight to him, learning to use her own newly-enhanced senses.

He stood once he saw her break from the trees and into the little clearing. Her dark, straight hair hanging loose down her back, her lithe, athletic body maneuvering over the terrain with little problem. She strode right up to him, paying no mind to his nakedness or erection.

When she stopped directly in front of him, he breathed in deep and drank her in with his eyes.

Her mouth set in a firm line, her dark eyes hard, she slapped him hard across the face.

Taken totally by surprise, barely feeling the sting from something like a human slap, he couldn't stop his head from flinging sideways. He would've done it anyway, just to give her some satisfaction. He deserved it.

Without a word, she flung her arms around his neck, raised up on her tippy-toes and mashed her lips against his with the same urgency he felt.

Lifting her to him, his erection pressed between them while they frantically explored each other's mouths. Twining tongues, licking at each other amidst little bites, Mercury couldn't get her close enough.

Kneeling down, he broke off the kiss to take off her shoes and pants while she wrestled her shirt off. There was no slow and gentle. There was no stopping to lave over body parts. He needed her here and he needed her now. And from her reaction to him, she felt the same.

Once she was as bare as he was, she again wrapped her arms around him and dragged him down to lay flat on top of her, hooking her long, lean legs around his waist.

She was wet and ready for him. He ignored his need to drive into her. Mercury needed to feel for the first time not only what a woman wrapped around him would be like, but, even better, his mate. He forced himself to stall at her entrance.

Dani rocked her hips up to him, encouraging his entrance. He moved forward just a little, his tip entering, barely fitting into her tight sex.

She moaned and tried to roll herself onto him more, but he kept himself steady. He would not ruin this by making his body's invasion uncomfortable, or even worse, painful.

He rested up on his forearms and locked eyes with his mate to watch this significant moment in their relationship play out in her expressions, not wanting to miss a thing.

Her chest heaved, her breasts arching toward him.

"Please," she gasped, "I need you inside me."

Mercury clenched his jaw and slowly slid farther in, fascinated at the slick velvet that held onto him so tightly, trying to draw him in all the way. He was big and wide, but it was like her body was made for him, he slid fully into her until he was encased in her wet heat up to the hilt.

"Daniella," he sighed, dropping his head into the crook of her neck. He wanted to pound away at her, take all the pleasure she could give and demand more. This was ecstasy. There was no pleasure before he was with her, only a tickle that was barely abated, and heaven within her. Absolute heaven.

When he moved back only to thrust forward, they groaned in unison. She grabbed his butt and at her urging, he let her set the pace through the pleasure-filled haze in his mind.

The pace quickened, he thrust in and out, couldn't get enough. Her pants and moans joined with his as they reveled in the feel of the other's body. Ecstasy. No wonder males went feral without a mate. Her presence soothed him, her body an outlet for his feelings and emotions. Their joining, a necessity for his very being. It wasn't just the difference between having real sex versus being on the receiving end of oral. It was her. There could never be another female for him, only Daniella.

"Mercury." Dani cried out, her nails raking down his back as she arched hers.

Mercury marveled at the feel of her walls quaking around him as her orgasm hit. He could feel each ripple, each tremor. He didn't have much longer and wanted to make sure his mate was well satisfied.

Dani grabbed his shoulders, riding out her peak, her heels digging into his butt. The sight of her crying out his name with her release, her head thrown back against the ground, her hair a soft dark halo against the grass, her breasts crushed beneath him, carried him to his finish.

His whole body tensed as his seed rose to release within her. He dug his fingers into the ground around her as he roared into her neck, body jerking and shaking, hot spurts jetting into her. Her body massaged every last drop out of him, greedy for his essence, though life from him had already formed within.

"My God, Mercury." Dani panted in his ear, her arms cradling his head, her legs still entangled lazily around his calves. "I had no idea it could be like that. Amazing."

Completely spent, Mercury could only nod his agreement where his head was resting in her comfort. Amazing.

Chapter Ten

They lay together, entwined in each other's arms dozing off and on between lovemaking sessions. The night was warm and any chills were staved off with shared body heat. Dawn had come and gone, the soft morning's light showcasing the beauty of their temporary love nest with its deep greens surrounding the light blues of the miniature waterfall.

It was beautiful here in the winter, but Mercury doubted he'd be able to bring Dani then. He propped himself on an elbow next to her, twirling his fingers across her belly. While flat now, it would soon swell with his child. Refusing to think of the role Sigma was playing in the growth and birth of their baby, he instead focused on the lovely woman next to him.

With a deep inhale, Dani stretched, eyes still closed. When she opened them, looking dreamily at him, she smiled. Then broke into tiny giggles.

Mercury gave her a perplexed look. Was it his beard and shaggy hair? It was only three weeks of growth, it shouldn't be wiry and sticking out.

"I totally punched your V-card," Dani said between giggles.

V-card? Oh. He was officially not a virgin. Mercury smiled back at her. "You punched it good."

"Sure did," Dani grinned. The light sparkled and danced in her eyes, her humor so genuine, Mercury knew he had made the right decision about her. She was no evil Sigma Agent. She was a young woman who made a bad decision and was trying to figure the rest of her life out because of it. And he would be there with her.

The laughter faded as she caught his serious undertone. "What are you thinking?"

He told her of his realizations and acknowledgments he'd had these past few weeks— truths about himself, about her, and they talked. She recounted everything, every detail she had given the other Guardians after he left. She even told him about the throat punch.

"I wish I would have talked to you first. I'm sorry I didn't," she confessed.

Mercury agreed, appreciating her apology. He had one of his own. "Sorry I took off. I just couldn't…" His brows drew together. Talking feelings was new territory and he found he didn't know how to be straightforward given the complexities of how he felt.

"I know," she said softly, cupping the side of his face gently. "Sorry I slapped you, but you totally deserved it after the first week."

Despite the seriousness of the situation, he smiled down at her.

"I did. They treated you well?" It was half question, half statement. He trusted his brothers with her. If she proved to be an evil Agent, they would have treated her as such while protecting the child. If she was genuine, they would have still treated her with caution.

"They did. If you can call a diet of twenty-five percent bacon 'well'." They both smirked at each other and his stomach growled at the mention of fatty, cured heaven.

With a grave note in her voice, Dani said, "Mason didn't make it."

"I know," Mercury said flatly. "I sensed it when I got to you. He attacked you and got what he deserved."

A beat of silence passed.

"His death bothers me." Mercury should have been devastated but he wasn't. The asshole intended to kill his mate and child. "He was never like the others, and with you and Cassie, he just hated humans. His hatred didn't make sense."

"He kept saying 'we'. Do other Guardians hate humans as much?"

Mercury thought for a bit. "No. A general distrust and wariness, maybe. When a human becomes a mate, they become part of the pack. Our mates are what we live for. Families are why we have Guardians. To protect the species from ourselves and humans. It just is."

Mercury's fingers trailed farther down from where they had been on her belly. His ever present erection around his mate pressed even harder into Dani's side. She rolled over to face him, stroking his hardness like he was stroking her.

"I should be sore, but I can't get enough of you." Dani leaned in for a kiss.

Alarms rang out in the form of howls, several shifters calling out. They weren't far away and were closing in fast.

Dani swore. "I forgot. I walked out of the cell. They must've found me gone and caught our scent."

Mercury popped up, grabbing Dani's clothes and handing them to her. She fumbled with the material, trying to get it right side out but it was damp from the morning dew and wasn't cooperating.

Nudity wasn't a problem for him, but it obviously bothered his mate to be seen naked. Without thinking, he sent out a mental order. *Stand down! Let her get dressed first.*

Dani looked up with a gasp. "How'd you do that?"

She heard him, too? Telepathy hadn't worked for the Guardians for a while. Well, it worked—sporadically. So much so, they went completely to radio contact. Like the rest of their gifts gone wonky, they'd quit using all mental powers, relying instead on brains and brawn. It was one of the reasons they were sent to bumfuck West Creek. At the time, their higher council didn't know

Sigma's tentacles had been so entrenched in this area. Or did they?

"Okay, I'm ready." Dani was fully dressed, her clothes rumpled and covered in grass. She resembled an earthen goddess with her dark hair and eyes complimented by the green hues around her, if earthen goddesses wore yoga pants and athletic shirts.

All right, we're ready, Mercury tried again.

He scented them before he saw them. Appearing amongst the trees around them were five wolves. Dani stiffened next to him when she saw them, well after he knew they were there.

The russet-colored big wolf transitioned silently into Commander Fitzsimmons. There was no need to explain what happened or why Dani had left. It was more than a little obvious when the smell of sex permeated their surroundings.

If the sex wasn't obvious, the new mating marks they each sported were. And freaking Sweet Mother Earth, the sex while being marked was… well, there'd be more biting.

The commander pinned Mercury with his daunting hazel gaze, concentrating internally.

Mind speak, came the order.

We need to go back so you can catch me up on what I've missed.

No, shit. This one from Bennett, who was still in wolf form. Well, hell. Mind speaking with four legs had almost never worked for them. Why now?

Why didn't anyone tell me we could do this? I could save a ton on my phone plan! Kaitlyn chimed in. She also remained in wolf form since she was still passing out after her transition back to human form.

The familiar furrow in the commander's brow told Mercury he had no answers either.

Let's go. Mercury, get Dani settled, and I'll talk to Master Bellamy before we meet. Commander Fitzsimmons transitioned smoothly back into his wolf as he left. Bennett followed with the twins and Kaitlyn retreated also.

Holding his hand out to his mate, he asked, "Ready to go home?"

***

Mercury settled Dani into bed after they showered. Although he couldn't stay and linger with her, he had pulled her into the shower after he shaved and trimmed his hair, and had his first ever, what Dani called, "quickie". He was an instant fan. Deciding against another round of sex while tucking Dani in, only because she was exhausted, he headed down to the lodge to meet with his team.

Bennett met him halfway there, as if he was waiting for him.

"You sure about her?"

"Yep," was all Mercury said.

"All we have is her word right now."

Mercury stopped and faced his partner. The male squared off with him, preparing for a physical confrontation.

"Remember when I asked if you were sure about Abigail and you said 'yes' but we both knew you were full of shit? Well, I'm sure about Daniella and we both know I'm not full of shit."

Bennett clenched his jaw and his right arm twitched. Mercury stood strong, readying for the blow but it never came. Bennett forcibly relaxed his body as a string of emotions carried through his expression. Anger passed into pain and sadness and settled on regret. Mercury noticed the deep shadows under his friend's navy blue eyes.

"What's going on, Bennett?"

"Nothing a visit to the club can't fix now that the twins are back in town."

"Watch yourself."

Bennett nodded and they hiked to the lodge.

Bennett's demons could ride him hard and things had been looking up, but Mercury suspected that watching a fellow Guardian find a mate was opening all kinds of raw, barely healed wounds within Bennett. Especially when Mercury's mate was willing to turn her back on everything she had known for years, because she both knew it was wrong and felt it was wrong. Bennett's mate had turned on him by turning him in.

Mercury also didn't think the club could fix anything, but it was in their nature to fuck, and to do it a lot. He also knew firsthand that getting off with random strangers didn't work any better than fighting or working out, or as Kaitlyn preferred, "power shop." But she, too, would give in rarely and head down to Pale Moonlight to use their special rooms, The Den. Only finding true mates would help, and in Bennett's case, the male was afraid lightning only struck once.

Making their way through the lodge to their intel room where Mason used to lurk, it seemed empty now, but brighter. It was as if the male's demise took away a darkness that had settled into the place where he had spent so much time.

Commander Fitzsimmons was leaning over the row of computer screens that showed interior rooms and the lodge's surroundings, along with a three-sixty span of the surrounding woods. Shifters had embraced the technology wave, so did Guardians—their pack especially. With their gifts on the fritz, they found much usefulness in today's information technology.

The commander wasn't one for small talk and he got right down to business. "We've been all over this place making sure Mason didn't set any traps. We found some bugs that didn't belong and replayed every angle available of his confrontation with Dani."

Punching a few buttons, Mercury watched that night play out all over again. Lights in the room flickered and one of the monitors blanked out.

"Calm down," the commander ordered. "It's over and done with."

Mercury envisioned his lovely lady tucked into his bed. The lights settled and the screens flickered back to life.

"I'll be damned," Bennett muttered. "How much of your gift can you control now?"

"Hard to say. It's not like we know what I can actually do." Never having complete control of his abilities made it hard to test their limits. After the debacle freeing Bennett at the turn of the twentieth century, he rarely attempted to use his gift. He used it to secure his cabin or open locked doors, but otherwise didn't want to hurt shifters or ruin missions in case it went awry.

"We'll worry about it later. We've done without it this long," the commander cut in. Nodding to the twins as they walked in, he continued. "What we need to figure out is who Mason was really working for. While you were gone," he pinned Mercury with a hard look, "we've ruled out everyone here being in on a conspiracy. At least this one." This time he pinned the twins with a hard look. They stared back innocently, as innocent as two full-grown shifters dressed in black leather, covered head-to-toe in guns, knives, and things that go boom, could look.

"Got any leads, Boss?" Malcolm asked. He usually talked for the both of them. Sometimes, Mercury wondered if Harrison could function without the other twin. The males were much younger than he at about fifty years old. Like him, they looked to be in their mid to late twenties.

"I do. And I'm not liking where it's going," the commander replied grimly. "Mason came to us before we settled in West Creek. Before that, he was up in Canada with a pack that worked directly for the Lycan Council."

"We know the council's dirty," Bennett said. "What about his old pack?"

A low growl from Harrison directed Bennett's scowl toward the quiet male.

"Yeah, I said it. They're fucking corrupt."

Harrison stepped forward and shoved Bennett who hit the wall with an oomph but rebounded quickly, barreling into Harrison with his shoulders. Both males hit the door hard and shook the whole room.

Mercury stepped aside, letting the males sail by as they whaled on each other. Malcolm almost looked bored, not as affected by the insult to his parentage as his brother.

"Enough." One sharply spoken word from Commander Fitzsimmons brought the two to a halt, chests heaving, adjusting gear and clothing.

"This is serious enough, we have to consider every angle. Since you two," the commander jutted his chin toward Malcolm and Harrison, "have close ties to the council, you're gathering intel and we'll start with what you already know."

"I wouldn't call the ties 'close'," Malcolm drawled.

"Our father wouldn't hunt and kill human mates," Harrison spit out.

"Now, our mother…" Malcolm said ruefully.

"Mal!" Harrison stopped to think. "Yeah, she might. But she'd do it herself."

Commander Fitzsimmons nodded. "Give us everything you ever heard growing up around council life, even if it's just rumors. Then head up there and gather what information you can."

"Got it, Boss." Malcolm saluted.

As he was leaving with his twin, the commander gave them one last order. "Off the radar."

"Always," Malcolm chuckled.

The commander turned to Mercury and Bennett. "While they're finding out who wants human mates killed, we need to find out why Sigma's using human mates to make babies. For what purpose, exactly?"

As if they didn't have enough problems.

"And we need details for Dani's doctor appointment."

"Is something wrong?" Mercury asked alarmed.

"Your mate needs to start her normal OB visits," the commander said. "We need to know if her pregnancy is progressing normally. We've got her in at the end of the week. You'll go in with her while Bennett and I stay outside the clinic. After the appointment, we'll go to the bank. We switched her accounts to us so she has the freedom to use her own money. We also moved her trust fund, wiped

out any old addresses, and got her stuff out of
storage."

"Have you told her that?"

"Nope. You get to." It was the closest
Mercury had seen of the commander smirking in a
long time.

Chapter Eleven

There were a few raised eyebrows at the handling of all Dani's remaining assets, but she finally just shrugged. "It needed to be done. When do I get my stuff? It's been years since I've seen some of that."

Mercury was astounded at the amount of money Dani had in her name.

Again, Dani shrugged it off. "My parents worked hard, saved a lot, and spoiled me. I was their only indulgence. After they died, I never had a chance to spend any of it. The only good that came out of me signing on with the devil."

"Jace transferred it, diversified it and some other shit I didn't understand, and left it up to you what you wanted for spending. We'll need to meet with him."

When they did, Mercury had become agitated during the meeting. Afterward, he confessed to little knowledge about financial matters and math in general, telling her he was never able to get beyond the basics.

She recalled seeing his scribbles in the cabin, but thought it was a hobby, like reading.

"I can help you, if you don't mind. But Mercury, it's not like I walk around understanding IRAs and annuities, either. I can't talk stocks and trading, that's why I hired out. I only need a basic understanding."

"But you've taken a lot of college level math classes. And aced them. I've seen your transcripts."

"I started to major in bioengineering because my mom pressured me to follow her, but then I had plans to be a big shot criminal lawyer, and the main reason was so I could wear power suits that cost over a thousand dollars each and be on TV. I couldn't do an algebra or calculus equation for the life of me."

"You were a straight A student."

"And I worked my ass off for it. But it's not like I use it every day. Or every year. Or since class for that matter. There isn't a whole lot I remember from my classes. If I worked with it, maybe it would come back. We aren't all walking math whizzes just because we went to school."

From the obstinate look on his face, she feared she wasn't getting through to him.

"Mercury. There's nothing wrong with your brain. Period."

Now they sat in the doctor's office. Dani was reading the latest in clueless parent literature the clinic supplied and Mercury was doing Sudoku. He wore a plain t-shirt and jeans, along with a baseball hat and glasses to help mute his exotic eyes. He was still insanely hot under his disguise. Other overly hormonal bitches in the waiting room must have thought so, too, as they eyed her man. Her chest constricted in possessive jealousy. She was about to engage in a few prenatal throwdowns, until Mercury gave her a quizzical look when magazines started rustling on the end table.

Dani decided once and for all that her mate—when had she began to think about him like that?—was undeniably attractive and she would have to get used to women noticing him. And God forbid they ran across any woman from his past at the club who would remember him. At this rate, Dani would throw the woman against the wall, not just books or magazines.

With a sigh, Dani calmed herself down. It hopefully wouldn't be this bad after the baby was born as it seemed the child added fuel to her raging hormones.

The clinic visit was anticlimactic overall. There were a ton of questions, many of which Mercury couldn't answer because they were family medical history questions, but once they told her doctor he was orphaned, it went quickly.

The pelvic exam proved more than a bit embarrassing, and this time it was Mercury asking all the questions: "What the hell is that thing?" about the speculum; "Does it hurt?" when the doctor inserted it; "What are you looking for down there?" Dani was extremely glad she chose a female obstetrician with a few years under her belt so

Mercury's astonishment wasn't the worst expectant dad behavior dealt with.

They both vehemently refused genetic testing, fearing the questions that would arise on the genetics they might find testing a half-breed. Dani reluctantly got normal prenatal blood work done, still fearing what abnormalities might get flagged, but worrying more that refusing the basics would raise even more eyebrows. Today was all about normalcy and blending in.

Sent packing with an armful of educational materials, free diaper samples, and another appointment in a month, Dani felt immense relief, yet more trepidation. It was still early. So many unknowns. This felt normal, but their baby wasn't and she didn't know what to do to shake off Madame G's tendrils.

"The bank's uptown," Mercury was saying. She'd been losing herself in her little world of anxiety, she almost missed what he said. "We can stop there and there's a drugstore a few doors down if you want to stop and pick up anything. As long as it's all clear."

"That'd be awesome." She felt downright civilized and it felt great being back in a world with appointments and errand running. Too bad she had to worry about being abducted and her baby stolen.

"It's daylight and in the middle of town, chances are low any Agents will try anything." Mercury tried to reassure her, as if sensing the road her thoughts went down.

Dani nodded absently.

The bank errand went fast. More signing papers, more women drinking in the sight of Mercury. He was oblivious and that was the only reason both he and the women remained unharmed. The stress of the day and the emotional upheaval left Dani feeling like her nerves were frayed, smoldering, and ready to blow. In her crazy uncle's words, her fun meter had been pegged.

The edginess increased as she wandered around the drugstore. Mercury must've felt the same way. He left her to shop with a quick kiss and he was gone to check the perimeter. He and the other Guardians were still using radio communication until they tested their telepathy more, not wanting to broadcast unintentionally right into an Agent's mind.

They'd given a few of her weapons back, but she wasn't wearing any. That would've been a little awkward during the doctor's exam, so they were stashed in her bag.

Mercury hadn't returned and she wandered as much as she could, finally purchasing some personal care items and, since she couldn't help it, a little lovey for the baby—a yellow scrap of the softest cloth attached to a fuzzy ducky head.

Now what? No Mercury and she'd already paid. She couldn't really keep wandering the store. She had to blend. What would a normal person, not hunted for their baby, do?

Dani headed to the front door. She could make it look like she was waiting for a ride while trying to catch sight of any of the Guardians. Her concern was mounting. Mercury had to have found something amiss if he wasn't back yet. Or maybe the other Guardians had run into trouble and were briefing him. Where were they?

Out of the corner of her eye, she spotted a sidewalk sign for the bookstore next door. What would it hurt? Sigma wouldn't look for her in a bookstore and she'd start giving off shoplifter vibes if she lingered here much longer.

Closing her eyes she pulled up an image of Mercury, Bennett, and the commander. Then she sent out a mental, *Heading next door to look at some books*. She hoped that if she did really pull off that mental trick, she didn't broadcast it the square block around the store to any being with latent telepathy talent.

Quickly ducking out of the drugstore and into the bookstore, she stopped to take in her surroundings. Exit to the alley in the back of the store, stairs to a musty smelling basement in the middle of the store, and an elderly man and woman manning the cash register. The only other people in the store were checking out and they didn't set off any of Dani's spidey senses. Cool, this shopping foray might not end badly.

Dani made her way to the end of the first aisle when she spotted a book. It was a new math tutoring aid that she thought might be more beneficial to Mercury than the ancient texts he was using. The book had many graphs and pictures, and catered to a younger audience that might be at the level Mercury was now. Dani squatted down to get a good look.

"Chick lit's in the next aisle, doll."

Shit! Dani flew upright face-to-face with Agent X, who was browsing through a random book pulled off the shelf. Oblivious in her browsing, Dani had wandered away from the front door, and away from the employees to where she could be easily cornered.

"Not that math can't get my girl juices flowing, but some of the new romance is pretty saucy." X put the book down and faced Dani with her hands on her jean-clad hips. Her raven hair was slicked back today showing off her buzzed sides and her belly-bearing shirt read Team Jacob.

"Mercury's here and so are the other Guardians, X," Dani warned. It certainly wasn't because X was the closest thing she had to a friend other than a few chats with Kaitlyn and Cassie at the lodge.

Regret flashed through X's eyes. "Doll, I know you're bluffing. We captured him out back. He's on his way to the compound now."

Disbelief rocked Dani. X was the one bluffing. Had to be! Mercury could not land in Madame G's hands. The things she'd make him do!

"You're lying," Dani challenged.

X's eyes flickered behind Dani and then back to her face. "You were the distraction today. They would be occupied with protecting you, not thinking one of them was our target."

Anger coiled in Dani's belly. The air electrified around her.

X's eyes flickered behind Dani again, an eyebrow quirked.

"Good thing, too. His claiming stench is all over you, but no matey-matey yet. That would've pissed Madame G off, wasting all that blood."

"I will kill you," Dani's voice shook. "And I will level that living hellhole getting him out of there."

"Are you sure you want to do that to me?" X's plump lips rounded into a pout. "After all I've done for you?" Her gaze once again went behind Dani.

Dani clenched her hands and glanced quickly over her shoulder expecting to see Agent E, or even the Guardians, closing in. Instead, books floated off their shelves and hung agitating in the air. The more her rage and despair rose, the more the books quivered.

That was her way out.

Dani turned back to face X, her face a mask of calm. "Who said words never hurt anyone." *Hit her!*

Books flew past Dani, so closely they lifted strands of hair. She spun a full one-eighty to sprint for the door.

Soft thuds and muttered curses followed Dani as X tried to run through the barrage of books hitting her.

Ignoring the shouts of the employees, Dani crashed out the door and sprinted to the end of the block.

Her chest heaving, she stopped to look around. No sign of Mercury, no sign of Bennett or Commander Fitzsimmons, no sign of Agent E, just a few people frowning at her dash to the corner.

Looking back at the store, Dani gasped. Standing just feet behind her was X, discreetly wiping her bloody nose with the back of her hand.

"Nice trick. I told the bookstore owners they better make sure to balance and level their shelves before I sue the shit out of them." X squinted into the partially clouded sun, drew sunglasses out of her back pocket and donned them.

"Now what, X? You take me out in the open?"

"Maybe if you ran out the back into the alley, but nah. There'll be other times." Her voice took on a grave tone. "But don't ever think Madame G will give up on that baby, not as long as her blood flows in it."

"What does she want a baby for?"

"Because she likes changing diapers and late night feedings. I don't fucking know. Find out what Madame G wants, then you'll figure out what she needs a baby for."

Squealing tires pulled Dani's attention away from the Sigma female in front of her. A black sedan she recognized as Bennett's came whipping up to the curb.

He jumped out and ran to her.

Dani looked back to the empty spot where X had been standing. Was the female's ability flashing? No, she had a form of mind control but was weak at it. Or was she? Dani was starting to suspect many more levels to X than the Agent liked people to think she had. And only vampires could flash. Dani never heard of a shifter having the ability, though they did have superhuman speed.

Turning back to the Guardian and seeing the blond's face filled with grim concern, she gave him the dire news. "They have Mercury."

***

Mercury woke to a draft chilling his bare flesh. Why was he naked?

Keeping his eyes closed, he opened his other senses up around him as he tried to remember why he was here and where "here" was.

An enclosed room. The draft must've have come from the female who just entered, the only other being in the room. He was stretched on a metal table, a wrist bound at each corner in silver cuffs, same with the ankles. The cuffs were the kind that severed limbs if they were tampered with. Well, shit.

Dani. Did they have her, too? He remembered giving her a kiss before going to check on the back exit of the drugstore. He'd felt uneasy, concerned Sigma Agents got past their surveillance.

The memories came back in a rush, his brain finally pushing past the mental fog of the drugs they'd shot him with. Seeing movement when he peeked out the back door, he was digging out his hidden radio to notify Bennett, who was the closest.

Then those bastards shot him in the back. Someone had gotten into the store and lay in wait. Mercury vaguely remembered the radio fumbling out of his hand, his mind trying to send out a mental SOS, but the haze had already settled in.

Inhaling deeply, Mercury scented the female. Young shifter female, probably less than fifty years old. There was fear residing in her, like it was a steady state of her condition. She also smelled…tainted.

Opening his eyes, he zeroed in on her.

Sensing he was awake, the blonde female met his stare, going from a bored fear to a sultry temptress in less than a second.

"Well, well," she purred, moving in on him. "I didn't mean to wake you."

Mercury kept his stare passive.

Seeing he wasn't immediately aroused, she straightened, attempting to make her bosom more pronounced. She wore a leather bustier attached with garters to sheer black stockings. Were those panties crotchless?

Comprehension dawned on Mercury. Sigma couldn't get to the baby via Dani, so they would attempt to make more babies.

"It won't work." He barely recognized his own gravelly voice, still groggy from the meds.

Mistaking his rough speech for passion, she sauntered up next to the table, leaning over so she was touching as much of his skin as she could, and palmed his manhood. Her hand cupped and rubbed as she licked a trail up his stomach.

He remained flaccid.

A perplexed look crossed the female's face. She doubled her efforts on him, massaging, manipulating, using both hands.

Not even a twitch.

Now she looked downright offended. Mercury smelled a spike in her fear.

"If I don't sleep with you, she'll kill me." The female's blue eyes watered with unshed tears. "You have to help me," she whispered desperately. One tear slid down her cheek.

"Madame G won't get rid of a shifter female who's been working for her for years," Mercury said flatly. "How long did it take for her to convert you?"

The female's face turned to stone, she put her hands on her hips and leaned in close, her fangs dropping as she hissed. "And when shifters turn to the mighty Guardians for help finding their lost little girls, how long do you look for them?"

Without hesitation, Mercury replied, "We never stop. We never give up. We will free you, if you want to be free."

The female let out a bark of laughter. "To be welcomed back by the clan that traded me for their security? No. I will take the power Madame G gives me instead."

"Being a fangbanger does not equal power."

She leaned in until her head was next to his. "If you do it right, it does." Her tongue rimmed his ear in one last attempt at seduction. Seeing the frown on his face, she pivoted to stomp out of the room.

"Female."

She turned to sneer at him, her hand hovering above the fingerprint pad to unlock the door.

"If you truly were traded to Sigma," Mercury said, "name your clan. When I get free, we will make them answer for their crimes."

She narrowed her eyes at him and turned away to drop her finger down on the sensor. The door clicked and unlocked.

Before the door latched shut behind her, he heard the words, "New Moon."

Chapter Twelve

"What do you mean we can't go in after him?" Dani was incredulous. "That's absurd."

Bennett hissed a sharp inhale and a little shake of his head to warn her off. Didn't work, Commander Fitzsimmons was talking crazy. *Fucking Guardians.*

The commander leveled her with a stern glare. "We're meant to police our species, not invade enemy territory. We don't have the manpower. The twins are up north, two of us are new, two of us are human—one pregnant—leaving me and Bennett. Even with Kaitlyn and Jace, it would be a suicide mission."

"What about Master Bellamy? Doesn't he have a mate?"

If possible, Bennett fell even more silent and dropped his head so low his chin almost touched his chest. The commander's jaw muscles ticked and his superhuman teeth probably cracked under the pressure.

"He's outta the game," he said finally. "Irina has no field training."

"But my new powers—"

"Are unknown and unpredictable." There's that stern, steady glare again as he patiently waited for it all to sink in.

They were screwed. Dani had seen enough during her brief time actually residing at the compound to know what they would do to Mercury. He wouldn't be the same if he ever came back, not if he spent any amount of time imprisoned there. Madame G wanted him to pay and wanted his semen. Tears welled up and threatened to spill. Oh God, aside from the torture, the morbid experiments, he would be made to—

"If you would've let me finish in the first place." Commander Fitzsimmons crossed his arms over his chest, the biceps bulging in their black sleeves, his piercing hazel eyes softening – just a little. "I brought you in here to talk about your telepathy."

Dani hastily wiped her eyes, nodded, trying not to sniffle on top of the tears. "That time in the woods was the only time."

"You told Bennett you tried to use it in the drugstore." When Dani nodded, he continued. "Mercury was probably already knocked out."

She shrugged. "I tried to project to both of you two, but it didn't work. I'm not a telepath."

"You're not telekinetic, either, but you mentally threw half a bookstore at Agent X. Whether it's a byproduct of the baby or latent powers coming awake, you may be the key to getting Mercury back."

***

Mercury was given a reprieve until another female entered, human this time. The scent... Mercury inhaled again to make sure... tainted. She was dressed like the first one, meant to entice him. Like the first one, it didn't work.

"She'll kill me," the girl whispered, tears streaming down her face.

Any pity he may have felt for the trapped human dissolved when she drew out a syringe and slammed it into his thigh.

Mercury twitched more from the shock of her action than that from any actual pain.

The human's lips curled smugly. "Resist the cocktail of love, Guardian," she taunted, pointing at his manhood. "In two minutes, you won't be able to keep that monster down."

Mercury kept his eyes trained on the drab ceiling, waiting for the effects of the aphrodisiac to kick in, while the recruit kept talking.

"When I took on this assignment," her finger trailed down his chest, "I only wanted to climb the ranks, even if it took growing a mutant inside of me. But you are delicious." She bit her lip, swirling her fingers around his side. "I will enjoy this mission."

That's right, little recruit. Keep talking. The more his captors thought they would win, the more information he could siphon.

"Madame G will never respect you after sleeping with a shifter. You'll get thrown back to the bottom of the pile."

The woman made an *oh please* face. "She's invested plenty in me. I'm invaluable."

"Keep thinking that."

The open-handed smack she gave his thigh echoed off the walls in the bare room. Mercury's eyes momentarily opened wide.

"You like it rough?" she purred.

"Maybe with the right girl. You ain't it."

That pissed her off, the echoes of the second slap louder than the first.

The fire from the drug curled its way through his body, threatening to make his mind hazy, trying to suggest the slender, brown-haired woman was like his Daniella. The thought of his mate was a lightning bolt to his groin, making his cock twitch. No more thoughts of his mate.

Forcing calm, even breaths, Mercury could have bored a hole in the ceiling with the intensity of his gaze. He drowned out the prattling of the woman, refusing to be distracted for even another tidbit of information.

Breathe in, breathe out. Think of cleaning up the recruit massacre at the lodge a few months ago. Think of scrubbing floors, replacing windows, dirty laundry.

The heat pressed harder, the woman was cooing into his ear all kinds of naughty sayings. His mate was not here, there was no reason to get hard.

Mercury kept that thought in his head as he closed his eyes, willing his body to burn off the drug faster. His metabolism spiked, tiny droplets of sweat broke out on his chest, the burning reached a crescendo, his mind fogging, threatening to lust for his mate.

Breathe in, breathe out. The coolness of the room began to seep into his body once more. The next breath out was a sigh of relief.

"I don't believe it!" The woman was one part incredulous, two parts pissed.

"I think y'all have a shit chemist." Mercury's voice was rough, betraying his cavalier attitude to hint at the extreme internal struggle he just faced.

She slapped him again, this time on the stomach, followed by another, and another. The slaps turned to punches, her screams of outrage echoing through the room. The beating didn't last long, she wore out quickly. It was more of an irritation to him than painful.

Her hair a mess, her lip bleeding from biting it, she stood back and huffed at Mercury and then stormed out.

Hours passed. Mercury dozed, sleeping off the rest of the drug; the cold metal table not as uncomfortable for him as his captors planned. There was no point struggling... yet. The silver would weaken him so he'd wait. Eventually, they'd release him; for a bathroom break, for transport, it didn't matter. He'd wait it out and make his move. His senses told him his Daniella was not at the compound, therefore he could be patient.

He sensed evil before the door opened. Well, shit.

This time there was no pretending he was asleep. He'd need all his senses for this.

The door opened and she walked in. Tall, with ink black hair pulled back into a high ponytail. Her hair was so dark, like it swallowed not only any light that hit it, but the life-giving essence of the air around it.

Madame G gracefully moved to Mercury's side, coming up even with his head. Deep, black eyes—inhuman eyes—stared down impassively. "You are making this difficult."

"Sucks to be you."

Displeasure rippled through her porcelain features.

"We are offering you a new start, with a new mate. One that isn't full of lies and deceit. I tried with a female shifter, but since you picked a human initially, I sent one for you to try."

"I have only one mate."

Madame G cocked her head, looking at him imploringly. "Do you?"

Hiding his confusion, Mercury held her stare. Still wearing absolutely nothing, still tied at each corner, yet Madame G never spared his body a glance. He was nothing but an experiment, an animal to be tested. A means to what end, and he needed to find out why.

"Daniella was quite the Agent, I hated to spare her for this mission. Her natural disgust of your species when she popped up on my doorstep was refreshing. She learned quickly how to kill your kind, performing each task with such zeal."

"Liar, liar, pants on fire."

Madame G drew back, surprised at his easy disbelief of her portrayal of his mate.

"If Dani was still your faithful Agent," he continued, "and you didn't fear your mission ruined, there would've been no need to bring me here." He lifted his hands as far as they could go in the cuffs, looking up at them. "Yet, here I am."

The tall, vile woman set her expression. "I will give you one more chance to give up your seed. Otherwise, I will talk to our doctor about going in after it."

She was turning to go, Mercury's words stopped her. "What will a baby net for Sigma? Power? Control?"

Madame G gave a derisive snort. "Sigma wouldn't know what to do with this kind of power," she spit out. "They are weak, their *grand* plan not grand enough. Why wipe out shifters when I can use them to rule the world?"

One last look of greedy disdain and she spun, heading to the door. Not a hair on her high ponytail even fluttered, the fabric of her standard long, blood-red kimono silent.

Mercury debated his next question. She wouldn't kill him, he was too important. They'd keep him strapped to this table, do unholy things, but not death. Not intentionally, anyway.

"What did you sell your soul for?"

Madame G froze. The light in the room seemed to dim, like an invisible vacuum opened around the dark lady, thinning the air, making breathing difficult.

As soon as it started, it was over. Madame G slowly turned back, moving with eerie stillness.

"What do you know of souls?" her soft voice half sneer, half innocent inquiry.

If he wasn't already tied down, he'd be pinned to the tabletop by her black stare alone. Her thin red lips in a firm line, her porcelain skin highlighted along the cheekbones by an angry blush. So Madame G wasn't impervious after all.

"I can see you are no longer in control of yours, sucking life out of the world around you." How else could he explain the effect she had on the very air around her? He lived for fifty years running in nature, surrounded by living, vibrant creatures. And then another hundred years working for his people, who sought to live in harmony with the earth and worship her blessings.

Seeing he was affecting her, albeit negatively, he pressed on. "Was it not enough? Is that why you need a baby?"

One long, slender hand lifted out of her robe, her fingernail colored black, transformed before his eyes into a long, tapered claw. She rested the tip against his shoulder, not breaking the skin. Yet.

"I do have a soul, Guardian," she nearly hissed. "It's growing in your little mate, dark and strong. Your baby is one third you, one third Daniella, and," the claw dug in and she slashed down to his navel, "one third me."

Mercury made a point of not flinching. Burning like salt had been dumped in the wound and washed away by acid, blood welled up and dripped down his sides. Madame G brought her claw to her mouth, displaying an impressive set of fangs, and swirled her tongue around the tip.

"Mmmm. They knew how strong you were. Did you know that?"

Mercury stilled. They? He had the feeling she was going to drop a big, stinky, can-I-believe-her, shit bomb on him.

"Your precious Lycan Council didn't know what to make of the clan with not only unusual abilities, but the rumors that they could choose their own mates."

"The fuck you say." Choosing mates? Ludicrous. Shifters sometimes waited centuries for their destined mates.

"Fuck," Madame G said flatly, sending chills skating over his skin at her seriousness. "Can you imagine the panic the council felt?" She continued, her tone smooth like silk. "The control they would lose? The social and evolutionary bounds shifters could make? They might start thinking for themselves instead of being cowed into submission for the benevolent, all-knowing council. Why, a mutt-blood might even land a spot on the council."

Madame G, rolled her eyes to the ceiling, in an uncharacteristic, overly dramatic display. "Could you imagine?" The forced awe in her voice barely left any room for the dripping sarcasm. "A clan with that power, and those abilities, coming to the attention of the terror-spawning boogey-man, Sigma."

Mercury's heart nearly stopped, anticipating what was coming next. Cold dread settled deeply into his bones and he willed her to just stop talking.

"Tell me, young Guardian? Would it be better for your council to let that clan fall into Sigma's hands? Or destroy them themselves?"

This time when she turned to leave, he didn't stop her.

Left alone in the silence, surrounded by the stench of evil, Mercury ruminated on the gut-twisting conversation. First of all, was the evil bitch telling the truth? He would scour this hellhole looking for any information she might have, even one word, about his origins, his family. To even know a name of someone from his childhood would give him an identity before he was the boy who was raised by wolves.

Secondly, it wasn't possible for shifters to choose their own mates. When he first saw Dani, covered in blood, taking on Agents with calm fluidity, he was smitten. She was badass. Then he smelled her and before his baby registered in his awareness, she smelled delightful. She smelled, like—

Well, shit. With mates, it was smell first, smitten later.

But he sensed her before that. Sensed something was wrong for weeks before he scented her.

Or was it the baby? Surely, she'd been in danger before with no awareness on his part.

Didn't matter. She was his and he wouldn't give up on ridding their lives of Madame G's influence. That meant first, figuring out a way to get her essence out of his child. Without killing him.

Him? Yep, Mercury sensed his baby was a boy. Strong and sturdy like his dad, athletic and intelligent like his mother. He wondered if Dani knew as much.

It'd always been that way with him. Was that one of the reasons his clan was decimated? He knew things about the world around him no one else seemed to notice. Not usually significant, he chalked it up to the way he was raised, spending all those years as a wolf.

His ability's increasing unpredictability caused him to not give it much thought, adapting instead to using his body and physical prowess. Once he was grounded by his mate and had a long conversation with Commander Fitzsimmons and

Master Bellamy, he would give more thought and effort to training his abilities.

Closing his eyes again, he thought of Dani. His Daniella.

Mercury. The dim echo of her voice made him wonder if he'd reached the point of hallucination.

Mercury. Now that was more than a dim echo.

Dani? It couldn't be. Their telepathy sucked. They'd warn the whole compound.

It's working! Bennett and Commander Fitzsimmons say they can't hear us so we should be private.

Where are you? No! Don't tell me, just in case.

Are you hurt? The concern from her strengthened him.

Just a scratch. I can't shift until they release the shackles. But they're coming to surgically extract what they're looking for.

Have they –? she broke off.

I've been slapped around by a few women, but my virtue is still intact. He felt her relief through their connection.

Is there a way for you to get out?

I can't change without these shackles taking a limb off. And they're silver.

Have you tried releasing them mentally, like your door and gun safe?

He never put those two actions together. The locks were probably similar. What a great freaking idea. But would it work, or take his hand off? The limits of his ability were unknown and they'd been increasingly unpredictable. After Bennett's rescue almost a century ago involving a keg of gunpowder and almost killing them all, he never trusted his control enough to practice, let alone use in the field. All the Guardians in the West Creek pack had similar stories.

Sensing his hesitation, Dani kept encouraging him. *Your cabin locks and safes are all mentally controlled. This is no different. Do you remember the layout of the compound?*

I don't know where I am exactly, but I'm guessing one of the lower level torture cells. It's not a monitored cell.

Those are on the east side of lower level two. Let us know when you get free. Her complete faith in his abilities humbled him and cemented his resolve. He would be free and in her arms by nightfall. Or daybreak. His sense of time was whacked underground.

And Mercury, I love you, so if you get killed, I'll be really pissed.

There he was, grinning like a bonehead alone in the room. *I love you, too, and will endeavor not to incur your wrath.*

You'd better not. There was a grin in her message. *Be safe.*

The connection broke, like a lamp going dark in his mind.

Centering himself from within, he expanded his mind out to the cuff around one wrist. He flowed around the cold metal, sensing any other forces at work. Feeling no spells or dark powers within the spring-loaded barbs meant to trigger with any major movement while the lock was set, he let his consciousness drift gently into the lock. It was a simple handcuff lock and all the locks worked off the same key. Cool beans.

Time to wait.

The lock clicked and the door swung open to reveal the most accurate stereotype of mad scientist Mercury could have imagined. The middle-aged human man with unkempt hair, wire-rimmed glasses, and a crisp white lab coat carried a tray of equipment. The equipment may have looked normal on any other tray, but since Mercury knew it was destined for his manhood, it looked pretty damned sinister.

The man set the tray down on a rolling table without sparing Mercury a glance, but never turning his back completely to the shackled male.

Snapping a pair of nitrile gloves on his hands, he then picked up a scalpel and vial.

Mercury jerked against his cuffs and smelled a spike in the doctor's interest. Sick bastard. To keep the show going, Mercury growled, baring his fangs.

"There, there. There's a good boy." The doctor's voice was low and soothing like he was talking to a raging puppy. "No worries, it's not silver. You'll heal and I'll repeat the procedure as often as needed."

The sick smile displaying yellowed teeth from excessive coffee drinking was filled with dark anticipation.

When the doctor's black eyes landed on Mercury's privates, there were four simultaneous clicks and the cuffs opened.

Mercury whipped one arm around the doctor's neck without leaving the table, spun him around using his other arm, and yanked. The neck snapped and the doctor's body went limp. The scalpel clattered to the floor.

A quick search of the man's clothing netted Mercury absolutely nothing but lint and nicotine gum. He would not leave here empty handed. Madame G would face dire repercussions for bringing a Guardian into her compound.

Recalling Dani's information about the layout and activity, and how she escaped, he used her exact same method. With the helpful doctor's finger to open doors, and blood to mask his own shifter scent, Mercury crept out into the hall.

A wall of doors lined each side, Mercury quickly inspected both directions. Recent signs of captivity assailed his nostrils, but no one inhabited the rooms. One scent sparked something familiar in

Mercury. It was recent—a young shifter, and he needed to be found.

That was all for the east side. Mercury headed to inspect the west. Now that he had more access to fresh air, he discerned it was the middle of the night, at least twenty-four hours since he'd been taken.

The west side was mostly empty but for two rooms. A male and female shifter, both in various forms of recovery from some sort of torture, were naked and splayed like Mercury had been.

Using the doctor's finger, Mercury opened the male's cell. His long, shaggy hair hinted at months to even possibly years of captivity. Baring fangs, he growled low at Mercury.

Moving to stand over him, Mercury looked the male in the eye. Seeing intelligence, and most importantly sanity, he determined the male could be saved.

"I'm going to free you and to get out of here, you need to do exactly as I say."

Taking in Mercury's scent, the male's eyes widened at the Guardian, then nodded imperceptibly. Mercury mentally unlocked the male's bonds.

When the male was freed, he stood and bowed his head, putting his fist over his heart. "Until I die, I, Garreth, pledge my service to you and your pack of Guardians."

"Let's hope that oath lasts longer than the next few minutes."

Next, they went to the female. In similar shape, the female appeared to have been imprisoned nearly as long as the male, maybe longer. As soon as the males entered, she snarled, snapped, and bit at the air, straining against her bonds. Her eyes were frantic and wild with fear. A pit formed in Mercury's stomach. If the female was feral, his only option would be to put her down.

Garreth moved to her side and once he captured her gaze, he held it. The female quieted, chest heaving but relaxed. He held her still with nothing but his eyes and gently touched her forehead. Without breaking eye contact, she slowly nodded.

"She will follow our commands, as long as we mean her no harm. Her name is Kerrice."

"You can mind-speak?"

Garreth shook his head. "I'm a healer of sorts. But she is my daughter."

"Is she feral?" Their situation was dire enough without having to face putting down the male's young in front of him, even though they both knew it was a mercy Sigma wouldn't grant her.

"Close," Garreth replied grimly. "I... I need to try to save her."

"As long as she doesn't endanger our escape, she comes with us. We need to make our way to the doctor's office. There's another male shifter prisoner I have to find."

"We'll follow you, Guardian."

Dani had been right. The compound wasn't heavily staffed, especially at night. The recruits were kept separate, and not allowed near the holding cells and lab. It was a nice advantage, and with no weapons, hell—no clothes—he'd take all the advantages he could get.

Heading to the stairwell, the three shifters crept up to ground level. Mercury knew exactly where they were and where the doctor's office was, and he couldn't wait to get there. Dani was right, the stairwell was creepy as hell.

Opening the door a crack, he held up a hand to halt the other two and let his senses roam. There were humans, the shifter he was searching for, and, Sweet Mother Earth, from the smell of fresh air—exits. Bet the big, important doctor had a nice size window in his office.

Bringing the beautiful image of his sweet mate to mind, he mentally reached out. *Dani, I'll be out in ten. Cover the doctor's window and plan for three extra rescues.*

Gotcha.

He turned to the shifters. Garreth was again calming the agitated female. "We can't get around the cameras up here. We're heading to an office, you two find as much data as you can grab, and I'll find the shifter. The window in the office is our exit." Waiting for their acquiescence, he finished, "Let's move."

Swiftly trotting down the hall, they maneuvered through the corridor, and using the mad doctor's finger, gained access to the office. Mercury cleared the room and was ushering Kerrice and Garreth inside when they heard shouts.

Fuck, it was on. They would have to fight their way out.

"Search it!" Mercury ordered slamming the door.

Garreth immediately headed to the desk, unplugging the laptop. Kerrice followed his lead, searching drawers. Taking stock of his surroundings, Mercury prepared to go out and take on the enemy to find the third shifter when another large window caught his eye. One-way glass.

Hastening to the window, Mercury peered into a dark room. Flipping the switch next to the glass, a light on the other side blinked on, revealing another room similar to the holding cell he'd been in.

The figure on the table moaned, turning his head away from the light. The shifter Mercury had been looking for lay in a heap on his side. The fact that he wasn't bound concerned Mercury. How bad of shape did the young male have to be in not to be shackled?

Gunshots sounded and the door shook. Not being able to open the highly secure office door, the Agents were trying to shoot the handle off. Maybe the assholes would run out of bullets before they blew it open, or get hold of something with more blast power.

Moving quickly, Mercury grabbed the office chair and smashed the glass to get to the young captive. After clearing the biggest shards out of the opening, he sprung over and into the room.

Jagged glass pierced his feet when he landed, but paying them no attention, he quickly went to the male's side. He was tall, but scrawny, no doubt starved. He had unusual coloring, in that he had very little coloring at all, except for the dried blood covering his body over the faded scars that would soon disappear completely. The experiments were recent, the boy would be out of it until healing was complete.

Heaving the young shifter across his shoulders, he barked, "Garreth!"

The older male had found the laptop bag and was loading it, but set it down to run to the opening. Slipping and sliding with bloodied feet, Mercury picked his way across and heaved his load to the other side of the window, doing his best to miss the remaining glass.

Once Garreth secured the captive, Mercury jumped back over just as the door was kicked in.

One man came rushing in, weapon pointed and ready to shoot Garreth, but Kerrice lunged for him, transitioning to her wolf midair, and taking him down by the neck.

Growling and screams filled the air as two more Agents piled through the door. To their disadvantage, they had the writhing bodies of the first Agent and Kerrice in the narrow doorway slowing them down, giving Mercury time to pick up the dropped weapon from the first Agent and take out another with a head shot. The third Agent moved efficiently around the first and got a shot off before Mercury got hold of him.

Searing heat laced through Mercury's shoulder. He'd been hit, a through-and-through. Ignoring the burn, he dispensed of the third Agent.

Motioning to Garreth to hand his unconscious load over, he ordered, "Out the window. Grab the intel."

Garreth hesitated, seeing blood draining from Mercury's shoulder, but finally hefted the shifter onto Mercury's shoulders.

Using the same method of window removal, Mercury swung the chair. It rebounded without even a crack. Son. Of. A. Bitch. Of course, they used bulletproof glass on exterior windows. If they could make it across the lawn to the woods, they stood a chance at freedom. It wasn't like they were getting out of the compound using the front door. They had to find a way to break the window.

Kerrice whined, still in her wolf form. The wildness was creeping back into her eyes. Even the staid Garreth was rattled.

Their heightened ears picked up the sounds of reinforcements heading their way. Zeroing in on the window, Mercury gave it a mental push. Sensing some give, he tried again, but harder. Still not working.

Dani, I need help taking out this window.

What do you need me to do?

Combine your thoughts with mine and we'll push it out.

Got it.

Concentrating on the window again, *Three, two, one!*

Energy poured through him and smashed into the window, flexing it outward until it eventually shattered out into the night.

Kerrice was the first to clear the opening, followed by Garreth, who transitioned before he jumped, the computer bag hanging out of his mouth.

Securing the unknown shifter, Mercury vaulted out, landing deftly on his feet, taking off in an instant run. He couldn't change forms and carry his load, consequently relying on his two legs to cross the expanse of the lawn.

Yelling and gunshots filled the air behind him. Return fire resonated from the woods. He hoped it was Kaitlyn on the long-range rifle. She was a crack shot.

Bennett's voice filtered through his mind. *Once you're in the trees, head west to the road. Dani and Jace are standing by with the vehicles.*

Flying over the grass, waiting for the fire of a bullet to slice him, Mercury made it to the tree line and kept going, waiting until he was well out of view to head west.

"Hand him over," Bennett's dark form popped up running next to him.

Barely slowing, Mercury passed the tall, gangly shifter off to Bennett.

"Who is he?" Bennett repositioned his load so he could run.

Dunno. It was easier for Mercury to use mind-speak, he was starting to feel the blood loss. *Garreth, you got Kerrice?*

The answering bark from behind told Mercury both shifters he'd rescued were on his tail.

"Our mission is to get the shifters and the information you stole back to the lodge," Bennett said. "We've gone from rescue to escape and evade. These woods are infested with Sigma."

Gunfire echoed through the night. The Agents shouldn't be able to see in the dark woods, but they probably had enhanced vision or night-vision goggles, or fuck, both.

A bullet tore through Mercury's thigh causing him to stumble. The stumble turned into a face first smash into the ground with a mouthful of dirt and tumbling to a stop only when he hit a tree.

Groaning, Mercury rolled to get up on all fours and attempt to stand, slumping his shoulder against the tree to push up when his injured leg wouldn't work. The burn of what felt like a million charley horses in his thigh told him the bad news.

"Silver bullet." Mercury's vision swam, the silver poison working faster with his blood loss.

"Fuck. Can you transition? It's only a mile to the road." Bennett knew Mercury wouldn't let him drop his load to help.

"I got him," Garreth's gravelly voice cut in.

He had the body frame to be big, like most male shifters, but his time in captivity robbed him of several pounds of muscle mass. Bennett gave him a dubious look, but it didn't slow Garreth as he hefted Mercury up, supporting his injured side.

Kerrice stood back, observing the scene. Her whines portrayed the urgency that they keep going, but also that as much as she wanted to help, she couldn't bring herself to get closer, much less touch the strange males.

Mercury's peripheral vision might be like looking through chicken soup at that moment, but he didn't miss the look of utter devastation and remorse that crossed Garreth's face whenever Kerrice made her mournful sound. He could only imagine the atrocities she'd been subjected to.

Deep in the woods, a sudden yell was cut off almost before it started. A quick howl told them why.

"The commander got one. We need to move." Bennett led the way, moving only as fast as Mercury's dead leg would allow.

You need to go ahead without me. Save the others.

Bennett snorted. "And deal with your pregnant mate when I show up without you. She's been a pain in the ass the last three days."

Three days?

"Yep. Time flies when you're having fun."

Mercury! What's wrong? Dani's sweet voice fluttered in his mind and he needed it so very much. Otherwise, the beckoning of unconsciousness was looking like a good option.

Nothing a little salt won't cure. And a few days of sleep. Care to join me?

Silver? Shit.

Yep.

If you promise not to die, I'll give you the most amazing blow job after you're healed.

Unconsciousness can go fuck itself. *Deal. But first, would you do me the honor of making our matehood official?*

Yes, now hurry your ass up.

Ah yes, his lovely mate had the heart of a warrior, not a romantic. Giving as much effort as he could, he and Garreth sped through the woods, following Bennett with Kerrice somewhere behind.

Detecting a road nearby, he caught Dani's sweet scent on the wind. It cut through the mental fog threatening to take him under as they cleared the remaining yards.

Dani jumped out of one of the SUVs and he was tempted to stop and stare. Her vibrant glow, even with the deep concern and fear for him in her features, was breathtaking. Seeing her with her hair secured in a tight bun, wearing all black, and loaded down with her weapons made three days feel like three years. Did the baby's powers help her get into his gun safe or had she blown it open?

Jace was standing at the driver's door. The shaved-headed male looked sinister before, but dressed in the standard all black Guardian gear, loaded for battle, his intimidation factor could be more effective than the weapons he brandished. "Get him in, we've got the jump bag ready."

"Mercury, oh thank God." Dani rushed up to him, ignoring their three new shifter additions, the injuries, and all of the blood, and grabbed his face to plant a firm, quick kiss on him.

Stopping much too soon, she pulled him toward the open door.

Climbing in fucking hurt. His leg could barely bend, but he managed to get his entire body in. Alarm shot through him when he heard two sharp barks from Kerrice.

Bennett, who was unloading the still unconscious shifter into the back of the SUV, whipped out his gun and faced the trees which Jace was already aiming into.

Even though she lacked the enhanced vision of the Guardians, Dani hopped into the back with Mercury, using the open window to aim her own weapon out.

Kerrice darted out of the tree line, limping with a crossbolt sticking out of her hind shank.

"Kerrice, get in." Garreth was opening the front passenger door for her.

The dark wolf hesitated, seeing even more strange males. Her amber eyes flickered between her father and the Guardians.

Commander Fitzsimmons silently emerged from the trees. "Load up. I got the Agent that hit her, the rest are back a ways, but one's a vampire and she'll get here fast. Bennett, we'll pick up Kaitlyn a few miles down the road."

Bennett ran to the other SUV along with the commander. Jace got in the driver's seat and put the vehicle into gear. Kerrice remained frozen.

"Kerrice, please," Garreth's tight voice betrayed his conflict. He'd made a pledge to the injured Guardian, but he just couldn't leave his daughter behind.

"Kerrice, whoever you are," Dani leaned out the window, "get the fuck inside."

The nose crinkled on the dark wolf as she measured Dani's scent. Finally, the she-wolf jumped in the seat. Garreth's sigh of relief was cut off by the door shutting as he ran around to crawl in the back on the other side of Mercury.

It was a tight fit. Mercury groaned when his leg was jostled by Garreth reaching into the front to grab the black duffle bag resting on the middle console.

"You said this was a first aid kit?"

"Sure is. Can you do anything with it?" Jace asked, looking in the rearview mirror at the older male.

"I have training, yes." Garreth was concentrating deeply, rifling through the bag, which consisted mostly of saline bags and gauze.

He grabbed a bag and ripped it open with one fang, handing it to Dani. "Pour this over his leg wound to help neutralize some of the silver toxicity."

She did as he asked, wincing when Mercury hissed in pain.

Garreth repeated his actions with another bag, handing it to her. "Same with this one, only slower. The bullet's still in him and this will help keep the toxin from spreading."

Dani followed directions and Mercury laid his hand reassuringly on her thigh, wanting her to feel no guilt for causing the pain that was saving his life.

Taking the gauze and clotting activator, he slapped both against Mercury's shoulder to stem the blood loss. Not even having the energy to hiss at the sting, Mercury let his head fall back onto the seat, allowing darkness to take him.

Chapter Thirteen

"Is he dying?" Dani asked the older
shifter, squeezed in on the other side of
Mercury. Trying to keep adrenaline from wringing
the saline bag empty in two seconds, she
concentrated on keeping a steady drip rate on his
leg wound. She heard that salt offset silver toxicity
but the idea to cart saline bags around was so
obvious it was genius.

"He's not well," the deep, cultured voice
rumbled.

Jace flew over the roads, maneuvering turns
that kept them clinging to their seats, Mercury
groaning, and the wolf up front digging her claws in
and finally getting down onto the floor, snapping
off the shaft of the bolt sticking out of her in the
process.

"Are you a doctor?" Jace asked, after
correcting a nasty fishtail around one curve.

The male reluctantly admitted, "Sort of."

"Close enough. Who's the dude in the
back?"

"No idea. We weren't allowed to see
anyone, only hear them."

Kerrice whined from the front.

Sigma bastards, Dani thought. *All of them.* Gritty, pointless, nasty torture was a hallmark of Sigma. Madame G used it to fuel her own agenda, no one, probably not even Sigma leaders knew exact details.

"And you never once tried to communicate?" Maybe just an innocent question, but Dani didn't miss a hint of accusation in Jace's tone.

"To what purpose? Increase the torture to each other? Or have it used against us even more?"

Jace inclined his head toward the dark wolf clinging to the floor mats. "She yours?"

"My daughter. I am Garreth. Kerrice, how is your wound?"

A little *wumph* from the front had Dani assuming it was a nuisance, but once removed, the female would heal quickly enough.

Silence filled the car until they reached the lodge, save Garreth checking vitals and changing bandages as they soaked through.

"Wait here." Jace was already outside the car, barely having flipped it into park.

Are you kidding? Dani wasn't sitting there to watch Mercury bleed out enough for the silver to finish him off.

Only seconds later, Jace reappeared with a stretcher as the other SUV skidded to a stop behind them.

Kaitlyn hopped out. "Sorry, we got delayed. But I got my first vampire kill. Rock on!"

"She'll never let me hear the end of it now," muttered Bennett, reaching in to help move the unconscious Guardian.

"I know, right? Cuz I was awesome!"

Mercury was loaded under the direction of Garreth, who transformed from haggard prisoner, to confident physician keeping keen watch on his patient. Dani trotted next to the stretcher, keeping her saline drip going. The Guardians hauled him inside to the infirmary, Kerrice limping, but sticking close to her father, and Kaitlyn in charge of the other unconscious shifter.

Numbly, Dani stood next to her mate in the infirmary, a room she'd never been in until now. A new saline bag was thrust into her hands before the old one had a chance to run out. Drip, drip, drip. Doc Garreth, as Dani thought of him, quickly searched the drawers lining the walls, grabbing what he needed—a scalpel and suture kit.

"We don't have time for finesse," was all he said, before pressing into Mercury's leg with the sharp blade.

Bennett and Commander Fitzsimmons watched Doc Garreth like a hawk watches a big fat mouse. One move in the wrong direction and they'd be on him. But Dani only sensed determination in the male to save his patient.

Saline mixed with blood and the stretcher was a mess. How Doc Garreth knew what he was doing she didn't know. In fact, she *didn't* know if he knew what he was doing, but at least someone was doing something to save her male.

With a clink, the bullet popped out of Mercury's thigh and tumbled to the floor, no one willing to touch it. Dani supposed she'd be on clean up duty of that particular fragment, one more small advantage to being human. Maybe she'd save it, find a way to mold it into a weapon and take out more Agents with it. Fitting.

Doc Garreth finished patching up Mercury's gaping wound from the inside out. "He'll have minimal scarring, thanks to the saline. You may quit now." He nimbly grabbed the bag from her and helped her to a chair to sit next to Mercury like he had much experience helping shell-shocked family around injured loved ones.

"Now, I shall wash and help the next patient."

***

"They're going to make you pay, dude. You bled everywhere." Bennett was giving Mercury shit about the rookies, Jace and Kaitlyn, having to clean up the aftermath of the rescue. "What really pissed them off was Garreth's bloody footprints."

"Not my fault he walked through all those glass shards," Mercury grumbled, still feeling rough. If a shifter was lucky enough to recover from the toxicity, the extreme hangover for days after almost did them in. Dani's warm body curled in next to his mostly uninjured side helped numb the pain while he rested on the uncomfortable cot in the infirmary. "Where's the commander?"

"Jace and Doc are filling him in on what they've found so far on the laptop. The mad doctor you killed was arrogant enough that he kept much more detailed notes than Madame G probably approved of. The thumb drive y'all grabbed was priceless."

"What'd it say?"

"I can't understand that shit,' Bennett said. "Garreth seemed to get it, though. He's crazy smart."

Dani perked up. "He has a Ph.D. in cellular and molecular biology. That's why Sigma wanted him—he worked for the Lycan Council. Apparently, they're a little more proactive than we thought. I gave him all of my mom's textbooks and notes from her genetic research. Maybe he can find a use for them."

Mercury snuggled his mate a little closer, relishing how her warmth chased away the lingering silver burn. "I thought he was a *doctor* doctor."

"Nah." Bennett chimed in. "He worked in emergency rooms as an aide for years, studying human medicine to bring the information back to his clan. That's how he was recruited by the Lycan Council and sent to school."

"So he checked out?" Mercury hoped so. He liked Garreth and he'd be a kick-ass asset to their team. But if they couldn't trust him...

"Check it, Mercury. He freely admitted to swearing himself to us to keep out of the council's reach. Like us, he suspected some dirty shit going down with those crusty old bastards and that's how Sigma got to him and knew where to find Kerrice to use against him."

"And how's she?"

Bennett turned grim. "Cassie's working with her, slowly earning her trust to help her."

"She'll be successful, no doubt. So now it's Guardians versus crusty old bastards?" Dani laced her fingers through Mercury's. He stroked his thumb against her silky, soft skin and tried to keep from imagining other silky, soft places he could touch. Didn't need Bennett seeing him tent his shorts.

"Haven't heard from the twins yet. I have no question they'll find any betrayal and how deep it goes. But they were ordered to stay off the radar and that'll be impossible once one of them opens their mouth and offends everyone in a three block radius. It'll take time." Bennett rubbed the back of his neck and stretched. He'd been hovering by Mercury's bedside almost as much as Dani. "Until then, we take down Madame G and go after the rest of Sigma."

"What about the young shifter I rescued? Talking yet?"

Bennett's mouth set in a grim line. "No. He only wrote his name, Parrish, and that he was sixteen. He's not deaf, but won't talk."

"Not even mentally?"

"Collapsed in the corner in a ball, rocking back and forth when we tried. I think we'll all need to learn sign language. Master Bellamy's working with him."

If anyone can get through to the kid, it would be the master.

Mercury thought back to the first sensation that rolled through him when he caught the young male's scent. "Anyone tell him yet?"

"That he's a future Guardian? No, Master Bellamy felt it was better to wait. Get him better, find out where he's from, and then start training." Bennett paused, his unfocused gaze on the wall like he was listening to something. "Duty calls. See ya, bro."

Mercury heard the same summons from Commander Fitzsimmons as Bennett. They were improving so much maybe they wouldn't need to text each other anymore. It'd make field missions pretty cake without the extra radio gear.

"Was I supposed to hear that, too?" Dani sat up, leaning over him, her hair brushing against his face.

He twirled the soft strands around his fingers. "Probably not. We're not sure how much we can hone our skills. Master Bellamy's theory is we're getting our control back as we find our mates."

She smiled a bit forlornly down at him. "I hope I don't lose too much after the baby's born. It'll be too hard to keep up with you guys."

"It'll be easier when we're officially mated. How about tomorrow?" Caressing the side of her face, he brought her down for a kiss.

Her lips parted in surprise at his question and he shamelessly used the opportunity to plunder her sweet warmth, sweeping his tongue inside. She instantly melted against him with a purr and stroked her tongue against his.

All too soon, she pulled back with a hand on his chest. "Are you up for the ceremony? Or more importantly," her voice dropped a husky octave, "the mating?"

Was he up for it? He'd been up for her since he regained consciousness, but her concern for him wouldn't allow him past first base. She said he needed to *rest* so he could *heal*. Then he had proven her right by passing out again.

"Let's practice right now."

Halting him with an infuriating hand on his chest, she gave him a placating look. "You still haven't gotten out of the infirmary. We're not having sex here."

"Okay. Let's go to the cabin."

This time when she stopped him with her hand, he snatched it off his chest and nipped at her palm, then licked over the nibbles, giving her his best puppy dog eyes.

When Dani's cheeks flushed and he heard the catch in her breath, he was ready to grab her caveman-style and head to their cabin.

"Three more days," she said firmly.

Son of a bitch! "Now."

Her mouth quirked up. "Two and that's final. We know the commander is ready to mate us and has the dagger thingy."

"Gladdus."

"That thing. And I'd like a nice dress. Kaitlyn volunteered to go out shopping for it. But most of all, I'd like you fully recovered."

"I can be fully recovered tomorrow."

"Not according to Doc Garreth." When he opened his mouth to argue, she talked over him. "I don't want to get cheated out of a ceremony. I want one thing between us to be traditional and proper."

Ah. Now Mercury got it. She needed the security. He was afraid when he filled them all in on Madame G's claims that he could choose his own mate that Dani was insecure despite her "Damn right you chose me" response. He was worried she'd lost confidence in them and would keep putting off their mating ceremony, but she was worried they would rush it and risk his healing, thereby risking their mating.

"Fine." He wrapped her in a big bear hug. One where she wouldn't feel pressured by being lined up with his ever present erection. "But once the ceremony's done, I will thoroughly pillage your body."

She relaxed into him. "Counting on it."

**

She was beautiful. The sun filtered through the trees, its rays landing on her, giving her an almost unearthly glow. Dani's dark eyes sparkled with affection and excitement, her chocolate hair swept up into a soft bun that he planned on releasing minutes after this ceremony was done. The feminine, lacy pearl-colored gown she wore with casual grace would be stripped off before her long locks could cascade over her shoulders. An imperceptible growl began deep in his chest at the thought of officially claiming his mate.

"Dude," Bennett chided, "can ya wait? I don't think Dani will care for the old way of completing the bonding ritual in front of witnesses."

Dani's eyes widened as the meaning sunk in, and Mercury scowled at his friend and partner.

Commander Fitzsimmons cleared his throat and the Guardians snapped to attention. Mercury faced his lovely mate. Other than the commander, they were the only ones on the porch of his cabin. The rest of the Guardians, along with Cassie, Irina, and Doc were below on the ground witnessing the ceremony. Afterward, they would filter to the lodge for a celebration that Mercury and Dani may or may not attend. Probably not. Mercury had plans.

Kerrice and Parrish did not attend. Kerrice was still leery of strangers and preferred isolation.

She agreed to intense counseling with Cassie and then planned to return to her clan despite Doc Garreth's apprehension. The pale-haired, pale-skinned Parrish preferred being alone with an Xbox, and since he was still mentally recovering, they let him be. Once they were all fluent in sign language, including Parrish, then it was game on and he'd start his training.

Commander Fitzsimmons recited through the vows, the revenant tone in his voice bespoke the significance of the act. A hush fell over the crowd as the ceremonial dagger was slid between their clasped hands and drawn back out smoothly and rapidly. Mercury gripped Dani's hand tightly, willing any pain to be absorbed by him as their blood mingled, bonding her life force eternally to his.

The small crowd waited with breathless anticipation while the ceremony drew to a close. When the commander said the final words, Mercury yanked Dani into his arms where his grin smashed into her grin, and they both laughed as they melted into each other.

Sliding Dani back down his length so they could suffer the delay of the congratulatory backslaps and handshakes, they graciously accepted well wishes from their closest companions before Mercury swung Dani up and mentally commanded his cabin door to open.

He quickly crossed the threshold with his bonded mate and closed the door to Bennett's "time to party" announcement. Going straight to the bedroom, Dani was already unbuttoning his black dress shirt.

"I thought that ceremony was never going to end," she said breathlessly.

"You're telling me," he growled, capturing her mouth again.

Tongues tangled while hands worked between bodies. She finished with his buttons, sliding the shirt back and down his arms, while he lifted her delicate dress up.

Somehow, Mercury managed to maneuver around hands aiming for the clasp to his pants, and tugged her dress completely off. He got a good look at his almost bare mate.

Holy. Shit.

How had she snuck those past him?

And would she be pissed if he ripped them off?

Pausing with the fly of his pants, which was proving to be difficult with the pressure straining against the zipper from behind, she looked up through her eyelashes at him.

"Do you like?"

"Fuck me. I likey."

The soft, satin swells of her breasts were cupped by a small scraps of lace with a fragile clasp in between that had an alarmingly low life expectancy. High and plump, her breast size already increasing with pregnancy, they defied gravity. The flimsy fabric was for decoration, its only functionality to incite painful lust in an already strung out male.

Eyes traveled down her toned, firm body to the even smaller scrap of white panties. He could see everything, but the material still symbolized a barrier to what he wanted most. What had been calling to him since he'd been taken. Almost two weeks, but it had felt like forever.

"These pants need to be off." Before she could tug at his waistband again, he ripped his pants off while devouring her feminine curves with his eyes.

Picking her up one last time before they settled in the bedroom for days, he spread her out on the covers, stretching out over her. Settling gently down on top of her, he noticed her bun was still holding together.

Reaching up, he plucked the hair tie out and fanned out the dark brown strands.

"You are the most beautiful creature I have ever seen." She was his. She left everything she knew for their child and trusted him with a life she held above her own before she even knew him.

"You're pretty magnificent yourself." Her hands roamed his body, obviously enjoying tracing the planes and ridges of his muscles. He aimed to please.

"But am I the *most* magnificent?"

Loving the twinkle in her eye, she laughed. "It's so obvious, I don't need to say it."

He nipped at her bottom lip. "I love you, Daniella."

She cupped his face with both hands. "I love you, too, Mercury Santini."

His new name rolled smoothly over her tongue. He finally had a last name. A name that wasn't made up just for him because no one knew his origins. A name he earned by getting the woman who blew his dreams away to fall in love with him.

Their lips met for a tender kiss. Her citrusy scent teased his nose and he had to have more. Kissing a trail down her neck, feeling her shivers under his hands, he blazed a path down to the useless lingerie snap. With a flick it was gone and her rosy peaks were bared for his mouth.

Her hands tunneled through his hair as his tongue traced each nipple, like he was committing every inch of her to memory. However, there was very little of her left that hadn't been permanently imprinted on his brain.

His mate was getting impatient, rocking her hips into him, and he continued his trail down to her delicious warmth.

Damn those few square inches of lace. One flick of his wrist and they were gone.

"You didn't like them?" Dani inquired innocently, but the huskiness of her desire told him she also thought they were better off.

"Fucking loved them, but they had to go."

Her sexy chuckle dissolved into a slight gasp when he used his tongue to tunnel through her feminine folds to find her most sensitive bud. She was slick, all for him. All his.

Drawing her bottom closer to him, he used his tongue to swirl her delicate nub down to her tight opening. He held her fast when she almost bucked up off the bed when he invaded her, tasting the molten honey her body was weeping for him.

Liiiiicking back up to her bud, he curled and nibbled while she cried out, but she was held firmly by him. She was so close to exploding he could have finished her in seconds, but wanted to prepare her for his body's ardent invasion. He was barely hanging on, his determination to please his mate was the only thing distracting him from releasing just as quickly.

Dani reached down and grabbed Mercury's hair when he slowly inserted one finger into her snug warmth. He slowed his pace to keep her with him and slid in a second finger.

Feeling her release his hair to clench the blankets, her pants and moans as she rode out his thrusts stoked his own fervor. Increasing the speed and friction of both his tongue and his hand, he carried Dani over the edge.

"Mercury!" she cried. Her body went taut for a millisecond before the tremors took over.

Her intoxicating heat convulsed and rippled over his fingers, leaving Mercury wanting to feel that sensation over his painfully enlarged shaft. Withdrawing, he crawled up over her.

"My God, Mercury. That was just—just—"

The intensity in his face didn't show the massive ego boost he received from her spent reaction. Positioning himself at her hot, wet entrance, he thrust forward with no pause until he was buried to the hilt.

Growling at the feel of her surrounding him, her body clenching and drawing him in as far as he could go, he paused only to let her adjust to his size.

"I wanted to taste you, too," she purred into his ear.

"Later. I need to be deep inside."

Hooking her legs around him and grabbing his face to bring him to her mouth, he thrust his tongue into her mouth with the same rhythm he set with his body.

Dani embraced him fully, hugging him even more forcefully. There was no way they could be physically intimate than they were now. He wanted every part of her.

Opening himself up, he gingerly cast out the depth of his love and pleasure to her.

With a gasp, she pulled back her head, awestruck. "I feel you."

The connection was open and he could feel her pleasure, and how it increased with each plunge. He pumped harder, feeling the hitch in her chest when the ecstasy intensified in them both. With one final surge, he let himself go.

Their cries combined as orgasm hit them both, finally easing some of the pressure Mercury had built up waiting to take his mate again. Her walls clamped down onto him, enhancing the pleasure as her body milked him until they both could give no more.

Mercury collapsed on top of his love, both of them breathing heavily, enjoying the afterglow.

"I love you," Dani murmured in his ear. "And I loved that."

A chuckled rumbled through his chest. "Then you'll love this."

At her delighted giggle, he began thrusting again, rubbing her with his thumb until she was ready for orgasm number three. Pounding into her willing body, he relished the feel of his woman taking his girth, moaning for more, and losing herself repeatedly.

Throwing his head back, roaring with the release, her legs wrapped around him, they both peaked together. Easing himself down to his side, he snuggled her into him with her back pressed to his chest.

She reached for his hand, weaving their fingers together. He repositioned her leg so he could push into her from behind.

"Mercury? Again already?" she asked, exasperated.

Using one arm to wrap around her and massage her supple breasts, he slid his other hand down between her moist heat. Pumping slowly, he only rested his finger on her swollen clit.

"Where do you think they coined the term 'mating frenzy'?" Feeling her melt into him, he wanted to beat his chest with pride.

"After this, we shower." Her breaths were coming quicker with his leisurely strokes. "Where I will suck you dry."

Groaning at the image of her on her knees, the shower's spray hammering at his back while she worked on him in front, he quickened his pace, his finger bumping on her most tender spot with each thrust. Within minutes, they were crying out together, his face buried in her neck, her face turned back toward him, as he filled her a third time.

Mercury gave Dani five minutes of afterglow and recuperation before he climbed off the bed, and grabbed her ankles to slide her down. Her surprised yelp switched to a jubilant laugh when he swept her up into his arms and carried her to the bathroom for their shower.

Chapter Fourteen

⊂Σ3⊃

Her nose tickled.

Dani roused from her warm nest next to the furnace she was now officially mated to. They'd fallen asleep curled into each other after the mating frenzy passed. Swiping at her nose, she felt something warm and slick. Swinging her legs to the floor, she sat up, feeling the drip fall to the floor. What the—

Heading to the bathroom with her head back and her finger under nose, she flipped on the light— a bloody nose. *Weird*, she thought. She'd only ever gotten her nose bloodied when she deserved it, like during training, not randomly.

She grabbed for a towel, when the cramps seized her middle. Dani gasped, doubling over, even looking down to see if there was a hot poker sticking out of her abdomen.

Before her knees hit the floor, Mercury was at her side, easing her down.

"What's wrong?" he asked alarmed. "I smell blood."

Dani tried to say something, but her breath was stolen when another cramp hit. Crying out, she grabbed onto Mercury's arm, leaving bloody fingerprints.

"The baby," she managed to gasp.

Both she and Mercury looked down at the same time to see dark red staining the inside of her thighs.

Bennett! Mercury roared mentally. *Dani needs Doc Garreth!*

Grabbing the towel and putting it between her legs, he swung her up into his arms, cradling her into his chest as she remained curled into the pain. Gasping between bouts of searing pain, tears fell hot onto Mercury's chest, mixing with the blood still dripping from her nose.

Rushing out of the bedroom, Mercury grabbed a blanket to wrap around Dani's naked body and snagged a pair of shorts and a shirt for himself off the nightstand by the door. Holding her tightly, Mercury sprinted out the door and down the trail to the lodge's infirmary.

The doctor met them by the door to quickly assess Dani. "Take her to a hospital. We aren't equipped for this."

Commander's got the car ready. Bennett rounded past them to hold open the lodge's back door so they could run through and out the front instead.

The black sedan was idling, with the commander holding the rear door open. Bennett went around to slide into the driver's seat while Mercury climbed in the back with Dani on his lap.

The commander's face grim, he nodded to Bennett and shut the door. Dani didn't need to look herself, affirmation was in the look of alarm fleeting across Bennett's face as his eyes flicked down to the blanket. She could feel the wetness between her legs, dampening the blanket.

The ride to town at illegal speeds seemed both excruciatingly long and alarmingly fast. In between the stabbing, searing bursts of pain, a dull throb settled into her lower belly.

This is it, she thought to herself. I'm losing the baby.

We'll get through this, Mercury calmed her, picking up her thoughts, and Dani was grateful. The pain was too bad for her to speak, but they still had a way to communicate.

The lights of the city flashed by as they crossed over to Freemont and sped to the hospital. Mercury settled her next to him only briefly so he could get dressed and then nestled her back onto his lap, whispering soothingly in her ear. She sunk into him, the anchor to her panic, grateful he was by her side.

Pulling into the emergency room's garage, Mercury pushed the door open and was climbing out before the car was fully stopped. The little elderly gentlemen staffed to direct the garage's traffic was pushing a wheelchair over for them, but Mercury blew by him, storming through the double doors.

An alarmed triage nurse looked as if she was going to try to stop them, but a quick look at the size of Mercury, and an even taller Bennett, had her faltering. Then her eyes landed on the now bloodstained shirt on Mercury, Dani's bloodied face, and the blood-soaked blanket around her.

"Follow me." She led them to a single room. When Bennett tried to follow, she hesitantly stopped him. "Are you related to the patient, sir?"

Bennett looked like he was going to push past her, but he glanced at Mercury instead. "I'll park the car and wait out front."

The nurse shut the door and began to gather information from Mercury and Dani, who was thankfully in the system due to her prenatal visits. Another young male nurse entered, donned a pair of gloves, grabbed some supplies and began to unwrap Dani.

It was a sign how scared out of his ever-loving-mind Mercury was that he didn't growl or lunge for the young man.

Dani tried to keep her breathing steady, concentrating on each inhale and exhale when the spasms hit. With each spasm, a little more blood seeped out between her legs and trickled out of her nose.

The next two hours went by in a blur. Mercury never left her side, holding her hand the entire time. They hooked her up to IVs, drew blood, checked her heart, performed an ultrasound and pelvic exam while Dani was in bouts of pain. They offered her pain medication, but she declined, unwilling to risk a mental fog during such a critical event.

There was a female doctor, not much older than thirty, who introduced herself as the OB/GYN on-call and had been in asking her questions, but Dani hadn't seen her since she was admitted.

Almost as suddenly as the pain came on, it stopped. Just suddenly ceased. Residual soreness remained, like she had done a killer ab workout, but no more searing, stabbing pain, nor throbbing or gushing blood.

Assuming it was over and their baby was gone, Dani and Mercury began the grim task of cleaning her up. The nurses had wiped quite a bit off her, but there was still dried blood and residue and she wanted it gone, if only to pretend their baby still had a chance. Grief clawed at her heart, but she remained resolute to hold it inside, until she was alone. Mercury's emotions roiled off him, matching her own. No she wouldn't be on her own; they shared this awful experience.

An aid came in to check on her and brought clean linens. Once Dani was clean, the bedding and her gown changed, her and her beloved sat to await the grim news.

"I still sense him," Mercury said, finishing bitterly, "but I can't tell if he's okay."

She remembered when Mercury asked her if she sensed their baby's gender and her delight when he told her they were having a boy. Tears poured down Dani's face when she thought she couldn't produce anymore. Mercury hugged her close, saying nothing.

A quick knock and the door opened. The young doctor gave them a small smile, carrying a little device in her hand. "I just want to check the heart rate again and then we'll go over the results."

Dani nodded despondently, dreading the anticipation of hearing nothing.

"Now, you're pretty early in your pregnancy yet, so we may need to do another ultrasound, but let's give this a shot first. Just don't be alarmed if I'm not successful," she smiled reassuringly.

Dani squeezed Mercury's hand and stared at the tiled ceiling. The cold gel was a pleasant sensation after the heat of her painful episodes. As the little wand slid over her belly, she heard static-like sounds that were of no consequence and a beat that matched her own heart. The doctor's brow furrowed, but she pressed on, making sure she thoroughly scanned both sides of Dani's belly.

The sound of a strong, steady rhythm filled the room with its rapid beat.

Smiling triumphantly, the doctor listened for a few seconds before removing the wand.

Unshed tears shimmered in Dani's eyes and she looked at Mercury, terrified to be ecstatic. His own brow creased, silver gleaming through his eyes, not clear on what the sound was.

"Is that—" Dani's voice caught.

"Your baby." The doctor was still smiling, relieved not to be delivering devastating news to the terrified parents.

"I don't understand."

"To be honest, I don't either." The woman pulled up a chair on the other side of the bed so she could talk to them both. "Other than being a little anemic, but nothing critical, you seem to be perfectly healthy. As for the baby, the heart rate was lower than normal when you first came in, but now it's sitting at a strong hundred and fifty-two beats per minute, which is perfect. All our other tests— perfectly normal."

She stood up. "My only instructions are to make sure you're taking prenatal vitamins, so you're getting enough iron, and to eat a healthy diet. Include a little more red meat and leafy greens until your hemoglobin level returns to normal. You'll need to have your doctor recheck your levels at your next OB visit. Otherwise, come right back if you start cramping or spotting at all."

"So, what happened?" Mercury looked as dumbfounded as Dani felt.

She shrugged. "We're doing some coagulation tests to see if you have a clotting disorder, but I don't think they'll be abnormal. Before she left, she turned and joked, "Maybe you didn't need all that blood."

Eyes wide, Dani turned to Mercury. Something Agent X said in the bookstore came back to her. *Madame G will be pissed she wasted all that blood.* The evil monster may have only needed a drop to bind her to a future baby, but months of growth would have increased the amount.

"Do you think our mating overrode Madame G's claim on me and our baby? Like our blood bond is stronger than hers?" She grabbed Mercury's hand and placed it over her barely rounded belly. "Do you sense her taint at all?"

Mercury closed his eyes, concentrating. When he opened them, relief and disbelief showed through the glowing, swirling dark silver depths. Slowly, a grin began to spread across his handsome face, showing off sharp white teeth, his fangs retreating.

Dani bit her lip, afraid to be happy. "Do you think it's the same for me? I'm not bound to Madame G anymore?"

"I never sensed her taint on you, but you swore a blood oath to her. Do you feel different?"

This time, Dani was the one who closed her eyes for inner reflection. Imagining that she was searching every corner of her consciousness, she floated through her own mind.

"I feel free." Disbelief quavered in her voice. "I didn't realize how shackled I felt, feeling that little bit of her inside me."

Mercury dropped his head onto her chest, expressed a sigh, with his hand still placed on her belly. "You two might be all right, but I don't think I will be after tonight."

Dani ran her hand through his short hair, watching the light reflect silver off the dark strands.

Lifting his head, he grabbed her hand, kissing the back. "Let's go home."

Epilogue

"You gonna go the planet route and call him Mars? Or wait, Saturn! That's a kick-ass name." The excitement in Kaitlyn's eyes was the only thing keeping her safe from Mercury's irritation. She was genuinely psyched, but spitting out naming themes and ideas for the last few months was getting a bit trying.

"No, Kaitlyn," Dani answered with a tolerant sigh, taking another bite of breakfast.

"Oh, right! Going the element route like Daddy. Maybe Barium, we could call him Barry." Acknowledging the eye roll, she kept trying. "No? Lead's hardcore. Oooh, Platinum! Yeah, maybe he'll have that funky color thing going on, too. Cool."

They were the only three eating at the lodge, waiting to start their day. Mercury planned to meet up with Bennett after the Guardian got back from an interview. They were going to go check out the clan the female shifter claimed sold her off for amnesty. It had taken them this long to gather the evidence they needed to not only prove her story, but determine if it was a widespread problem. Their findings were disturbing.

"Can we put her out of her misery?" Mercury grumbled around a mouthful of bacon.

"Okay, Kaitlyn. Our official name announcement, just for you." Dani grinned wickedly, almost feeling bad at Kaitlyn's giddiness. They had told the others weeks ago, but kept Kaitlyn guessing. The female seemed to enjoy all the names she could come up with.

"What is it? What is it?" She squealed with delight.

Of the entire pack residing at the lodge, Dani should have guessed Kaitlyn would be their biggest cheerleader. The Guardian was full of a zest for life and anyone around her couldn't help but ride on her coattails. She had even started buying baby gifts. Excessively. Dani had to ask her to hold off or they would run out of room.

Rubbing her now rounded belly, also Mercury's favorite pastime—well, second favorite—she gave a dramatic pause.

"We've decided to name him after my father for the middle name, and keep an Italian first name."

Kaitlyn clapped her hands together, nearly jumping up and down, her long braid swinging behind her.

"Dante Antonio Santini."

Kaitlyn threw her hands up. "Perfection!"

She leaned down to give Dani a hug, then gave Mercury a noogie while he scowled, hiding a smile.

"Oh, Dani, you're cooking for me tonight, right?" Kaitlyn asked. "I mean, I don't want you to go cross-eyed staring at screens all day."

"You're so considerate," Dani said, with teasing sarcasm. "Yep, lasagna. My grandmother's recipe—extra meat, of course."

"Hell, yeah. Catch ya later, bitches." Kaitlyn left with a wink.

Dani loved rotating the more domestic duties into her week between learning the security and computer systems. Mason's death left an opening and now she could be like the rest of the Guardians. Finding a niche she realized she had a passion for, Dani dove into learning everything electronic. It kept her busy when missions took Mercury away from the lodge for days at a time.

Once she had a good handle on that, she planned to work on cool experimental gadgets. She'd be like James Bond's Q, noting with irony that she just referred to herself as a letter when she never did with Sigma. Q probably didn't have a playpen or bouncy chair in his lab, though.

"Ready to get your techie on?" Mercury stood and held out his hand to help her up.

Dani looked at the male who had become not only her mate, but her partner and best friend.

"Let's do it."

***

Bennett narrowed his gaze on the deranged young man before him. Ratty honey-blond hair stood up in tufts as if the man in the metal gray scrubs constantly tugged at it. The round, padded room was a drab white, no color to be found. Only a shabby mattress on the floor and one blanket decorated the entire room. The man's entire existence—brought down to one room and a blankie.

Bennett agreed to talk with the guy because of details he revealed during a psychotic breakdown in Cassie's office before she was ever introduced to their world. Fresh out of school, struggling to build her practice, she'd had no doubt this patient needed to be committed after hearing his ravings. He was a danger to himself and others.

Fast forward six months to when she learned about, and became a part of, the world of vampires and werewolves. She remembered young Ronnie Newton and his ravings, and realized the guy may have been serious, and in great danger.

Agreeing that a Guardian needed to talk to the young man, Cassie arranged an appointment to meet with Ronnie, only to find out he was not only in psychiatric isolation, but was restricted from receiving visitors. No problem—Cassie was his therapist prior to commitment.

Big problem. For some reason, security was a major issue and it was extremely difficult to get to Ronnie Newton.

Bennett looked into the kid's background and found nothing exceptional, except the fact he didn't exist. Made sense—who the fuck went by "Ronnie" nowadays? Bennett always made sure his name stayed current and trendy. He predicted "Bennett" would carry a few decades. Benji didn't need to exist anymore. Bennett Young left that shit in the past.

So, here they were. A drugged-up kid, all of twenty-two, with no past, squinting at them through his drug-induced haze. Cassie was talking in low motherly tones to keep him calm and determine how much mental status he could reach in this conversation. Jace waited outside the door using his magic eyeballs to keep staff from getting too concerned about their presence.

"Do you remember what you said that day in my office, Ronnie?" Cassie ventured.

"You didn't believe me. You gave me to them."

Bennett's eyebrows rose. Well, well, well. Tightened security for safety reasons, or Sigma trying to prevent the Guardians from finding out what this kid knew?

"I'm sorry, Ronnie. I really am. I believe you now."

Ronnie made an indignant sound. "Do you? Or are you just trying to find out what they want to know?"

"We want to help," Cassie countered.

"I knew you'd be with them." He titled his head toward Bennett. "You finally brought them here."

Did he have special abilities? *Well, I'll be damned.* Bennett finally caught on. The kid was good. "Why fool them into thinking the drugs work on you, but not pretend with us?"

Cassie looked questionably between Bennett and Ronnie, the irritation at being interrupted fading away as comprehension of Bennett's claim dawned on her. "You're one of us?"

Ronnie leaned forward so quickly Bennett prepared to take him down if he lunged at the woman. Jace would be a pain in the ass if Bennett let the man touch one fiber on her.

"You're fucking crazy!" But his eyes told Bennett a different story. His eyes remained calm, lucid. "Do you think I'd be here if I had any skills that could get me out? Sorry, just a puny human here."

Cassie's gaze flicked to Bennett, making sure he was on the same wavelength. "So then why do they want you?"

"They think I know where *she's* at. Or that she'll come to me once she finds out I'm in this place."

"She?" Bennett asked.

"My sister. They think she's the alpha hybrid. The one that will give rise to a new species. One that can't be conquered by vampires or shifters. One that can finally live on Earth without hiding."

Bennett and Cassie sat in stunned silence.

"But they're wrong," Ronnie shrugged. "It's not her. Whoever Madame G is selling her soul to for world domination fucked up."

"Why do you think that?" Bennett couldn't help but be caught up in the kid's story, suddenly wanting every detail on the mysterious sister. Finally, they were getting some answers on Madame G's goals. Were they both hers and Sigma's? If Ronnie was telling the truth, was Madame G led astray, and about what and why?

Ronnie's expression froze. "I just know. Besides, why would my sister be key, but not me? If she's a hybrid, then I would be, too. And if we were hybrids, would we really have all the strengths of both species and no weaknesses? Doubt it, there is no such thing as an alpha hybrid. Perhaps we could blend better, but most likely, we'd take on the traits of one species or another, like how offspring of human mates are shifters. So why do they want her?"

Ronnie rocked back on his mattress hugging his knees as Cassie and Bennett absorbed his ponderings. Bennett tried to read into what the kid was trying to tell them. Ronnie's sister wasn't the alpha hybrid. And if she was the first ever offspring of a vampire/shifter mating, what would the big deal be? Maybe a territory conflict over who would rule the poor soul?

"Seriously. At least you saved me Doc. If I wasn't locked up here, I'd be at Sigma's compound getting milked dry while they tested my sperm for shits and giggles."

"Then I don't understand why you are here and not there?" Cassie mused.

Ronnie shrugged. "Dunno. What do flies and minnows have in common?"

Bait.

Perplexed, Cassie asked, "Why are you talking to us?"

"It's nothing they don't know already and you're the good guys. It's about time you're getting up to speed. Besides," Ronnie pinned Bennett with bright hazel eyes, absolutely not clouded by anti-psychotics. "You need to find her."

Thank you for reading. I'd love to know what you thought. Please consider leaving a review at the retailor the book was purchased from.
Marie Johnston

Also by Marie Johnston

The Sigma Menace:
Fever Claim (Book 1)
Primal Claim (Book 2)
True Claim (Book 3)
Reclaim (Book 3.5)
Lawful Claim (Book 4)
Pure Claim (Book 5)

New Vampire Disorder:
Demetrius (Book 1)

Pale Moonlight:
Birthright (Book 1)

About the Author

Marie Johnston lives in the upper-Midwest with her husband, four kids, and an old cat. Deciding to occasionally trade in her lab coat for a laptop, she's writing down all the tales she's been making up in her head for years. An avid reader of paranormal romance, these are the stories hanging out and waiting to be told, between the demands of work, home, and the endless chauffeuring that comes with children.

Sign up for my newsletter at:
mariejohnstonwriter.com

Like my Facebook Page Marie Johnston Writer

Or follow me on Twitter @mjohnstonwriter

Printed in Great Britain
by Amazon